WOLVES OF THE BEYOND

BEYOND

LONE WOLF

The Outermost

Cougar
Tree

Cave
Before
Time

BEYOND
THE
BEYOND

MacT
Terr

Frost Forest

Winter den
of Thunderheart
and Faolan

Summer de
of Thunderh
and Faola

Salt Lakes

N

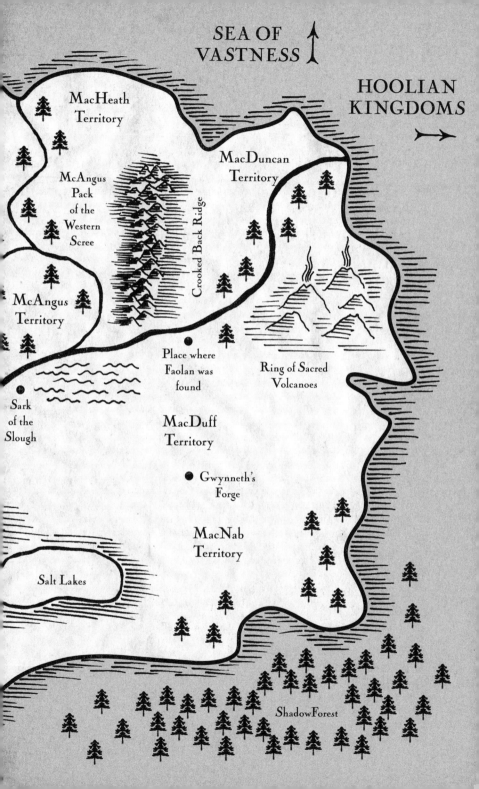

SEA OF VASTNESS

HOOLIAN KINGDOMS

MacHeath Territory

McAngus Pack of the Western Scree

MacDuncan Territory

Crooked Back Ridge

McAngus Territory

Sark of the Slough

Place where Faolan was found

Ring of Sacred Volcanoes

MacDuff Territory

Gwynneth's Forge

MacNab Territory

Salt Lakes

ShadowForest

KATHRYN LASKY

WOLVES OF THE BEYOND

LONE WOLF

SCHOLASTIC PRESS / NEW YORK

Copyright © 2010 by Kathryn Lasky
Interior illustrations by Richard Cowdrey
Interior illustrations © 2010 Scholastic Inc.

Library of Congress Cataloging-in-Publication Data

Lasky, Kathryn.
Lone wolf / by Kathryn Lasky. — 1st ed.
p. cm. — (Wolves of the Beyond ; #1)
Summary: Abandoned by his pack, a baby wolf with a mysterious
mark on his deformed paw survives and embarks on a journey
that will change the world of the wolves of The Beyond.
ISBN: 978-0-545-09310-1
[1. Wolves — Fiction. 2. Fantasy.]   I. Title.
PZ7.L3274Lo 2010
[Fic] — dc22
2009017007

10 9 8 7 6 5 4 3 2   10 11 12 13 14

Printed in the U.S.A.   23
First edition, January 2010

Map illustration by Lillie Mear
Book design by Lillie Mear

"And in our wolf language the word *Hoole* simply means 'owl.' You see, my friend, it was the spirit of a Hoole that I followed when I led my kind here from our ice-locked land."

— From the first book of the Hoolian legends

CONTENTS

PART ONE

THE BEYOND

AWAY . . .

BEFORE SHE FELT EVEN THE FIRST twinge in her belly, the she-wolf set out to find a remote birthing den. She knew somehow that this birth would not be the same as the others. She had been traveling for days now, and she could sense her time was near. So far she had seen nothing that would serve as a den. There were several shallow pits, but those wouldn't do. Pits offered no shelter, and though it was almost spring, the weather could turn treacherous in a flash. The pups could freeze. The sound of their fresh hearts beating so fiercely would grow dim under a thin glaze of ice until the hearts stopped, and there was only silence. This had happened before to the she-wolf. She had licked those three pups until her tongue was dry and bleeding from the cold shards, but she had not been able to keep up with the ice.

This was her third litter. And this time, she knew she had to get far away from the pack, away from the clan, away from her mate, and most of all, away from the Obea.

Finally, on the night of the fifth rising moon that now hung like an ice blade low on the horizon, she found a crevice under a rock ledge. She smelled it before she saw it. The scent of fox was distinct. She hoped it wasn't a whelping den. *Just the fox, dear Lupus.* She sent up a silent prayer. She did not want to contend with fox kits.

And it had been just a fox — a fox waiting to give birth. The she-wolf routed her and took the den, settling in for her time. The fox smell lingered. *Fine,* she thought. It would provide another layer of concealing scent. She rolled in the scat that she found nearby and then snorted to herself as she imagined what her pups would think of their mum. No matter, they would live — and if need be, live away from the clan.

Then they came. Three pups, two tawny like their father, the other silvery gray. They were perfect in her eyes. Indeed, it took her a while to discover the one little flaw on the silver pup — a slight splay to his front paw. When the she-wolf examined it more closely, she saw that this paw had a dim tracery of a spiral, like a swirled star, on its footpad. It was odd, but certainly not a deformity.

And she told herself the splay of that paw was minor. He was not *malcadh*, the ancient wolf word for "cursed." It was such a slight flaw, and she had hope that the splay might lessen in the days that followed. The toes that pointed out might rotate back, and the tracery was so dim it wouldn't leave a print even in soft mud. The silver pup was strong. She could tell by the way he sucked on her teat. Still, she was glad she had taken the precaution of finding a birthing den far away.

She dragged the pups one by one into the deeper recesses of the crevice, which thankfully had two or three tunnels that extended into a nesting chamber. Here she planned to stay wrapped around her pups for several days, nursing them in the quiet darkness as long as she could. She knew that soon enough they would become restless, and when their eyes finally opened, they would seek that pale thread of light that gleamed feebly at the den's opening, drawn to it as strongly as they were drawn to the milk from her teats, as strongly as they would later be by the scent of meat. But if they could remain concealed, they would survive and the silver pup would grow stronger and stronger so that the threat of the Obea would begin to fade, like an old scent mark scoured away by wind and rain and snow.

The she-wolf would have only a few hours for such fanciful thinking.

◎

In a world that to any other wolf might appear trackless, Shibaan, the Obea of the MacDuncan clan, had found the she-wolf's trail. The laws of the wolf clans were harsh. The Obea was the female wolf in each clan designated to carry deformed pups out of the whelping den to a place of abandonment. Only barren she-wolves were eligible, since such wolves were assumed not to have developed maternal instincts. With no blood offspring, Obeas were devoted entirely to the well-being of the clan, which could not be healthy and strong if defective wolves were born into it. The rules were precise. The deformed or sick pup was to be removed by the Obea and carried to a remote spot where it would be left to die of starvation or be eaten by another animal. If the pup somehow managed to survive, it was permitted back into the clan as a gnaw wolf and became the lowest-ranking wolf in the clan. A *malcadh's* mother was never welcomed back. The clan must be rid of her and her mate, who had contaminated the bloodlines. If they were to survive, they must separate and seek new lives in different clans, for they were deemed to have destinies marked by blight that might be set right only by finding new bloodlines.

Shibaan had learned to become suspicious when a pregnant female about to give birth went *by-lang*, which meant "deeply away." She was an experienced Obea and was not fooled long by the tricks of the she-wolf Morag. Shibaan had to admit that Morag was more thorough than most in covering her tracks. Morag had not urinated except in streams or the ice-free parts of the river. She had left no scent marks to declare her territory. The average wolf would not have noticed the clues to the desperate mother's flight. But Shibaan was no ordinary wolf, nor was she an ordinary Obea. She found the subtlest of traces. A tuft of silver fur caught on some thistle. Scratch marks on a rock that had served as a foothold when Morag crossed a stream. A slight whiff — a scent message perhaps, not from Morag, but another. To Shibaan, it flared up like a signpost. The message was clear: *My territory, first lieutenant of the MacDermott clan*, a response to an outsider veering too close to MacDermott land. *So,* thought Shibaan, *Morag has crossed the MacDermott border. Daring!*

Then there was the scent of fox, but not pure fox. Shibaan shook her head wearily. *I always find them, no matter what tricks they play.* And she did. The fox scat outside the den even had a thread of fur, like a silvery pennant quivering in the breeze to announce that inside a she-wolf concealed herself, sticky with fox scat, but still redolent in the sweet fragrances of new pups and warm milk.

No fuss, no muss. The mothers of *malcadh* never did put up a fight. They knew the consequence of resistance — immediate death to all the pups.

Morag watched the Obea carrying the splay-pawed pup in her jaws until they were a dark speck on the horizon. How perfectly suited Shibaan was for this job! It was as if the years of performing her duty with unquestioning obedience had scoured away any kind of feeling or imagination. When Morag looked into the green eyes of the Obea, they were completely devoid of light, or depth, or anything that might reflect emotion. They were like dry stones, bleached of nearly all color.

The silver pup had allowed itself to be picked up by its neck scruff and had instinctively curled its body into carrying position. Did he not sense the Obea's scent was different from his mother's? Did the pup not mind the milkless, dry, sterile wind of her being? The pup had nursed constantly — but constant had been just a sliver in the short day since it had been born. The pup's eyes and ears were still sealed shut. It would be days before they opened. The pup's only way to know his mother, the Milk Giver, was through her scent and perhaps the feel of her fur and the throbbing rhythms of her heart. Would he remember? But what did it matter.

A tween season storm was brewing, and these were the worst. Coming on the edge of spring or the cusp of summer, tween storms were full of rage, tumultuous winds, and slashing ice. Morag had felt it coming and seen the leaden skies sinking lower and lower, clamping down on the land like a trap for earth's creatures. Her pup would be abandoned in the midst of this storm. And she herself would have to remain with the two other pups to await the Obea, who would return to lead Morag back to the clan. The Obea would carry one pup and Morag the other as they traveled that trail of shame. The news of the *malcadh* pup would be announced, and Morag would have to leave the clan immediately, an outlaw. The surviving pups would be nursed by another wolf.

The Obea, though lacking imagination, did have thoughts. Practical thoughts. Where should she take this pup so that there was no chance it would survive? She had seen something on the pad of the splayed paw that disturbed her. She wasn't sure why; all she knew was that she had not liked those markings.

What Shibaan *did* know was her job: to take care of the bad business of the clan. She did not mind her duty now. Long ago her failure to have pups was like a sharp pebble underfoot, a constant reminder that she would never be a mother but instead an unranked wolf charged with an unpleasant task. However, she performed her work well, and over the years she had gradually gained some respect from the chieftain. The sharp pebble, once an irritation, became smooth and settled in her being like a polished river stone — there not as a reminder of failure, but simply as part of her character, her charge, her duty as an Obea.

As she carried the pup, she glimpsed again the odd spiraling mark on its footpad. She felt a tremor in her heart. She could have killed the pup, but the Obea was very superstitious. It was against the law to take shortcuts, and she wanted to climb the spirit trail to the Great Wolf, Lupus, and the Cave of Souls.

Ahead, Shibaan saw the gleam of the river under the gray skies that pressed down. It was there she intended to leave the pup. The river was just beginning to break up in the spring thaw. And when that happened the level would rise suddenly, torrentially, and the pup would drown. She would leave it on the edge, where it would be caught by the surging waters.

She arrived at a spot where the bank had been undercut by the course of the river. There were already signs of thaw, so she placed the pup on an ice ledge. It was a spot certain to be swamped, especially when the storm rumbled in.

The Obea was careful as she put the pup on the ice — heedful, precise. The pup was an it, neither a he nor a she, nor even a wolf. Just an *it* that squirmed, mewling and whining weakly. But all that would be over soon. If the storm didn't take the pup, an owl would. The river was on a major flight path of collier owls who flew into the Beyond for the coals spewed from the volcanoes. They were always hungry when they got to this point. This *malcadh* would not be the first seized by an owl from the kingdom of Ga'Hoole. There were smith owls, too, that set up temporary forges near the volcanoes. Smithing was hard work. Those owls ate a lot. Despite the close relationship between owls and wolves, a *malcadh* was fair game.

There was a *tick-tick* sound as the pup attempted to grip the cold, smooth surface with its tiny paws. The mewling and whining escalated to weeping, but the Obea didn't hear it. Her ears were sealed as effectively as the pup's. There were no vague stirrings deep within her. If anything, she felt only the cold, smooth weight of that stone that had become synonymous with her duty, her charge, her identity. *I am the Obea. That is all I need to know. All I need to be. I am the Obea.*

CHAPTER ONE

THE RIVER ROARS

HE COULD NOT SEE, HE COULD NOT hear, and vainly he poked out his tongue to lick, but the smell of milk was gone and with it the warm teat. He could feel only cold, nothing else. It filled him until his small body was racked with violent shivers. How had everything changed so fast? Where was the stream of warm milk, the soft fur, the squirming presence of the other pups? In his brief life, he had known little, but now he knew less. Smell, taste, and feeling, the only senses he had, were starved. The pup felt himself drifting off into a void that was neither life nor death, only a terrible nothing. And with this great void came numbness.

Something stirred — a vibration — and with it a new element entered his barely pulsing life. The terrible cracking and booming as the river ice buckled was so loud that it penetrated the pup's sealed ears. Then suddenly, a roar surged through his head. There was a great lurch, and he began to skid off the ice shelf, but digging in his sharp little claws, he gripped hard.

It would seem a cruel trick that the lone pup gained two vital senses, sight and sound, as the winter-locked river ruptured and broke free. It was perhaps the shock that caused his eyes to unseal and his ears to open.

The final thaw of the river unleashed immense cataracts of water that tore at the banks, uprooting trees, dislodging boulders and rocky outcrops. The shelf on which the Obea had placed the pup creaked, then tilted, and at last, there was a sharp crack that splintered in his ears. Light flashed brutally in the pup's eyes as the moon scorched the ice floes sweeping down the river.

Dim in the pup's memory was a previous violence. Birth. He had been launched from the warmth of his mother's womb into the grip of forces greater than himself. His small body was nothing against the intense contractions that expelled him. And now it was happening again. But instead of going from the inviolable warmth of his mother's womb, he was sliding into the frigid waters of the tumultuous river. He dug harder with that splayed paw, which seemed to have a better grip than the others. He clung, clung dumbly to the shelf that had joined the other flotsam in the river.

It would have been easier, less painful, to release his grip, to slip off and drown. But there was only instinct, and the instinct was to grip. He opened his eyes wider and saw the gleam of the full moon on the river. The brightness made him squint.

His first lesson: He could adjust his eyes to the light. His first thought: What else might he adjust or be able to change? Might he bring back the warmth he once knew? The smell of milk, the taste? The soft crush of those wiggling furry creatures that had tumbled about him as they all scrambled for the milk? The comforting rhythmic vibrations he felt as he pressed close to suck? There was something beneath the fur, deep in the Milk Giver, that beat.

Icy water dashed over him, but still he clung. Occasionally, he felt the ice shelf spin round and round in one place. The light swirled and he experienced a dizzying nausea. To steady himself and keep his grip he had to shut his eyes tight. Then there would be a jolt and his raft would break loose and join the tumult of the stream again. He felt the ice diminishing beneath him. His hind legs hung off the raft now and were growing numb in the water. The numbness crept through him. It was not an unpleasant feeling, but with it something else seemed to grow dimmer, to seep from the deepest part of him. His claws began to lose their grip.

The last thing he felt was a tremendous jolt; the last thing he heard was the sound of his claws skidding across the final fragment of his ice raft.

CHAPTER TWO

THE SPARK
FROM THE RIVER

ON THIS STORMY NIGHT, THERE
was a sound that rose louder than the roar of the river
and the howling of the wind. The anguished cries of the
mother grizzly shook the banks on which she sat. Her
great gulping grief seemed to suck the air from the earth.
The long guard hairs on her back were sheathed in ice
and trembled, creating a bristling litter of small sounds
beneath the rage of her grief.

When the river had threatened to flood her den, she
had turned her back for a few seconds to scan for higher
ground. In those seconds, cougars had erupted out of
nowhere and made off with her cub. Her single cub. She
had only grown one this time. All summer and fall
she had eaten, fattened herself up, and for what? To have
what would most likely be her last-born killed.

Now, with her teats still dripping with the milk meant for her cub, she was ready to die. She welcomed the river that she had hoped to escape. Not since the mating time five summers before, when a male grizzly had killed one of her cubs to get near her, had she grieved like this. She would not move from the den where she had birthed and suckled the cub. She tipped her massive head toward the moon that watched her like a dead eye, and pleaded with Great Ursus, *Take me, take me!*

The grizzly had lost all sense of time, but the night became darker as the moon slipped down in the western sky. Near dawn, the storm had blown out, leaving dark clouds on the horizon like smoldering ashes. The river flood had reached its peak, but still had not taken the grizzly.

A dark sodden clot snagged on her half-submerged hind leg. She shook her foot at the annoying scratching sensation. But when she shook, the clot clung tighter. It made her irritable, and she dragged her paw up onto the bank.

She would later wonder what it was that stopped her from reaching forward and simply scraping off the clot. It betrayed no sign of life. The scratching could have been the prickly thorns of a bramble that had become entangled with the flotsam of the racing currents. River trash. That was all. And yet she felt something.

She would think of it as a spark. She had seen sparks come from the sky, and sparks struck from rocks when tumbling boulders collided, but she had never imagined a spark coming from a river. A spark from a river, unquenched, undamaged, undiminished, flying upward from the watery turbulence and containing in its minuscule sphere of light, the promise of life. So she reached forward and carefully picked up the sodden clump with both her front paws. It didn't squirm. She couldn't see signs of breathing. But it was a cub of some sort, and when it opened its eyes with what seemed great pain, she *saw* the spark.

As the sun lifted over the horizon, she saw its light reflected in the cub's two eyes. And then she saw an image that shocked her. It was her own reflection in the eyes of an animal that was not born of her, nor of her kind. *It's a wolf,* she thought. *I seek death, and it seeks life.*

And then she looked up at the sky, searching for the Great Bear constellation. She could not see it, for dawn was breaking, but deep down she knew that this wolf was a message from Ursus, a scolding. She must not think of death. Her time had not come yet. It wasn't an accident that the pathetic pup had fetched up on her leg. It was a gift from the river.

"Faolan," she whispered. "I shall call you Faolan." *Fao* meant both "river" and "wolf." And *lan* was the word for "gift."

"You are my gift from the river." And she gathered him to her chest.

The Milk Giver? The pup smelled the milky traces in the thick fur and nuzzled toward the source. But the closer he got, the more confused he became. It did not seem the same. The smell was different and the taste as well. And there was a new, frightening sound. The thunderous roar of the river was replaced by a great rhythmic booming, and threaded through the mighty reverberations were gusty bubbling sounds. As the grizzly gently pressed Faolan closer to her teat, the sounds actually shook him. Yet he felt safe.

It was a different Milk Giver. A huge one, many times bigger than the first, and he was hearing the pumping of her heart and the turbulence of her stomach. Gradually, he became used to the sounds. They blended into the rushing of the river, folded into the quieter noises of his own sucking.

He sucked. His world became one of milk. Thick rich milk. He shut his eyes and slept, still sucking.

The grizzly looked down on Faolan and huge tears rolled from the corners of her eyes. *The river spirit brought you to me. There must be a reason. I shall nurse you through this morning into the day and through the night. A spark can become a flame, a flame a fire.*

She blew her warm gentle breath onto him. The pup's eyes fluttered, and he sank deeper into dreamless sleep.

CHAPTER THREE

MILK AND LIGHT

THE PUP MIGHT HAVE BEEN SENT from Ursus, and the grizzly might have had the best of intentions, but she was at a loss to imagine how she might take care of this pup beyond nursing him. He was a greedy little creature, that was for sure, and he was so different from a bear cub. He smelled different. He sucked differently. And although he was a bit larger than a newborn bear cub when she had found him, he was not fattening up as fast. A bear cub would have doubled its weight by now. The wolf pup had grown some, but not enough. And yet he nursed incessantly. The grizzly worried that her milk was not right, or perhaps she wasn't holding him properly. What did she know about raising a wolf pup? If he had been a sign from Ursus, there should have been more signs. Signs that told her what exactly to do.

The grizzly told herself every day that the pup was a gift. But she wanted him to be more than just a gift. Did he feel she was strange, too? *But what do cubs know?* She was startled and nearly chuckled. *I called him a cub!* And then she realized that even though the pup was a wolf, perhaps they were all alike. *Cubs, pups. They think about nothing but milk. Faolan is no different.*

He had paused in his nursing for a moment, and she took the opportunity to pick him up in her huge paws and hold him close to her face. They peered into each other's eyes. His were becoming a lovely green, like the wolves' eyes in the Beyond, and hers were a rich, gleaming brown, so shiny that the tiny wolf could see his reflection in them.

"You're a funny little creature!" And she stuck out her tongue and dabbed his wet little nose. He gave a happy *yip yip.*

"Oh, you like that!" She did it again, and he squealed now with delight.

She set him down. He immediately rolled onto his back, holding his tiny paws in the air expectantly. The grizzly thought this was a signal that he wanted some tickling. She began to speak with a mixture of words, snorts, and huffs. She wasn't sure if he understood her or not. It didn't matter.

"Oh, Great Ursus, you want me to do this again, you funny little fellow."

The words of the wolves and the bears and the owls did not differ much, but the tone and the expressions in the subtler movements of their heads or their eyes created a hidden language strange to other animals, and sometimes incomprehensible.

Faolan lay on his back, waiting for the huge tongue to tickle his belly. So she did. And the pup leaped up gleefully. This was repeated several times. Then the pup ran a distance and turned his head to look slyly back at her. He suddenly hurled himself toward the grizzly, leaping into her arms. She was so stunned, she fell backward. He climbed up her chest and began licking her chin, then her nose.

The bear's chest rumbled with chuffs of delight. The more she chuffed, the more Faolan licked her nose. The bear felt her eyes fill with tears. For days this wolf pup had nursed but had hardly seemed to look at her. But now, now when he had finally stopped nursing for just a moment and she had played with him, he played back. He understood. She picked him up again gently and held him away from her face.

They peered once again into each other's eyes. He wiggled a bit and made the *milk! milk!* bark. She cradled him, and he clamped on to her teat. But this time there was a difference. He opened his eyes as he nursed and looked right at her. It was as if there were a current flowing between them. Faolan consumed the milk, and the grizzly drank in the luminous green light of his eyes. She felt a deep surge of love.

CHAPTER FOUR

THUNDERHEART

THEY MADE A CURIOUS TWOSOME —
the great lumbering grizzly with the sun reflecting off the silvery tips of her brown fur, and the small pup, his coat a brighter silver, scampering sometimes ahead of her, sometimes at her side, sometimes behind as they foraged for the spring bulbs that were just pushing their sprouts through the ground. One would grunt and the other would yip or hurl out snappish barks. Yet somehow they had found a way to begin communicating. Faolan had begun to swing his head exactly like a bear cub would when saying no.

More and more the grizzly realized that rearing a pup was not all that different from rearing a cub. She marveled at the similarities between the two. Yet it frightened her how small Faolan was in comparison to bear cubs. Small and defenseless. However, the pup was very fast, much faster than a bear cub, and could cover ground with great bursts of speed. The grizzly thought Faolan's speed might compensate for what he lacked in size. But there was the problem of his splayed front paw, which he favored. A wolf, just like a bear, needed full use of all its paws.

Faolan now had begun to lag behind and was making small whimpering *I'm tired* sounds. The grizzly turned around and glared at him. Faolan whimpered and squatted in a hummock of soft grass, wagging his head and growling. "No, no, no!" he said, then blew a great spray of air through his nostrils as if to proclaim *too hot!*

He walked slowly forward as if he could hardly drag himself to the grizzly's side, and nudged against her to try to clamber onto her back. There was a huge muscle over the grizzly's shoulders that powered her forelimbs, and Faolan loved to climb aboard and ride high on it. Bear cubs were too large to ride at this stage, but not the wolf pup. Even in the den, Faolan liked curling up on that furry mountain when he wasn't nursing.

Having mothered three sets of cubs, the grizzly had heard all the complaints before. And it really didn't matter if they were bears or wolves, the young got tired, they got cranky, they wanted to go back to the den and nurse — easy food. But one day the grizzly's milk would dry up, and the pup would have to learn about other sources of food. It was particularly important for Faolan because he was so small. *Is he small for his age? Perhaps this is the size of all wolf pups?* the grizzly wondered. Nonetheless, it made her nervous.

It surprised the grizzly that she had grown so attached to the little one. But that spark she had detected when he had first fetched up on her foot and opened his eyes seemed to kindle throughout his tiny body. He was quick, smart, very strong willed, and now the fires from the spark sometimes had to be tamed. How could such a tiny little thing contain such fierceness?

The grizzly lumbered up to Faolan and butted him with her boxy nose. He tumbled backward, squealing in mock pain.

"Get up," she grunted.

"No! No!"

"No" was most definitely Faolan's favorite word. "No" and "More milk." It sounded slightly different when he said it than when bear cubs uttered these same words. His voice was higher, not as deep as a cub's. The grizzly wondered if this was because his chest was so much smaller than a bear's. It was so narrow, so fragile. His growls were also shallower than a bear cub's. However, the accompanying gestures were very similar to those of a cub. Did the pups of the wolves' packs toss their heads about this way? From what little she had seen of full-grown wolves, their gestures were nothing like these. Once she had watched a pack from behind a huge boulder as they tore at the carcass of a moose. There was an elaborate formality to their every move. Certain wolves ate first and then others crept up as if requesting permission to partake of the meat. She wasn't sure how they would deal with a whining, obstreperous pup like Faolan, who had just flopped himself on his back and was flailing his splayed paw dramatically.

He wanted to go back to the den, to the cool, welcoming shadows, to its earthy coziness, to the smell of the river, to the soft moss pads that grew at the opening where he loved to take his morning nap. But most of all, he wanted to curl up against the grizzly and nurse. Even the thought of that sweet milk made his stomach growl. Bulbs had a horrible taste. There was no juice in roots. He had even complained that they were too hard for his teeth.

He began whining loudly now.

"Urskadamus!" The grizzly grumbled the ancient bear oath, which meant "curse of a rabid bear." Then she blasted him with a series of short huffs of intolerance.

This was the first level of scolding. But Faolan continued to whine and roll on his back, wagging the splayed paw.

Enough of this! she thought. *He must learn not to give in to his weaknesses.* He must, she realized suddenly, learn to make them his strengths. It would be a cruel lesson, but there was an even crueler world awaiting him.

She growled for the first time ever at the pup and then with her own mighty paw whacked his good front paw. Now Faolan howled in real pain. His green eyes flooded with astonishment. *How could you? How could you?* he wondered.

The grizzly did not have words for every occasion that a young pup would understand. Sometimes teaching or communicating by example was the best way, and then later the words would come. So she lumbered past Faolan and began digging in a patch of onion grass with her own paw, the one she rarely dug with. The message was clear: *Use the splayed paw! Make it your digging paw.*

Meekly, Faolan began to scratch the dirt where the onions grew. It took a long time, but finally he dug one up.

The grizzly was proud. She came up beside him, making low purring sounds, then nuzzled him gently and licked Faolan under his jaw with her enormous tongue. She turned and began digging in another nearby patch of onions. Faolan stared at her in dismay. *More?* he thought. But he began scratching with the splayed paw. He did not want to risk her wrath again. What would hurt more than a whack was if she said he could not nurse.

No milk, only onions! Unthinkable! He dug harder.

The pup had done well. The grizzly had watched him out of the corner of her eye. In a very short time, he had turned the splayed paw in a special way so that he could get nearly the force he had with the other paw.

Faolan was a quick learner, and not just quick, but inventive. Still, the grizzly constantly regretted that she knew so little about wolves. But bears and wolves tended to avoid one another. This was quite different from the owls and the wolves, who had formed a close alliance over a great span of time that reached back to when the wolves had first arrived in the Beyond. The grizzly often thought that if she had been an owl, she would have been a better mother to this pup. But it was stupid to waste time regretting that she was not an owl.

Instead, she thought and thought, searching for every

scrap of memory she had of wolves. She vividly remembered once watching from a high promontory two packs that had come together to hunt. She had been quick to see that the way wolves hunted was very different from that of bears. Bears were much larger and more powerful, but wolves made up for their lack of power with their clever ways. Bears never formed packs. And perhaps because of that they had a different manner of thinking. The wolves' ways seemed complicated and mysterious.

And owls, the grizzly continued her musing, *owls are so clever!* They knew how to make tools, weapons. They stuck things in the fires of their forges and made claws that fit over their talons. Perhaps, she thought suddenly, bears weren't so smart because they were so much bigger, bigger than wolves and so much bigger than owls. Then a really dreadful thought occurred to her: *Perhaps I am not smart enough to rear a wolf pup!*

She looked back at the poor little thing as they made their way to the den. He was completely exhausted, wobbly to the point of staggering off the narrow path. He was most likely too tired to even cling to her hump while riding. *Well,* she thought, *smart or dumb, I'm all he's got.* She turned around and picked the little pup up with his head in her mouth and the rest of his body dangling, the way she would have carried a one-moon-old cub. At least two moons had passed since Faolan had fetched up, and he was still small enough to be carried carefully in her mouth.

Tomorrow they would make their way an even longer distance to forage for the squirrel caches of white bark pine. The white bark that squirrels used to line their nests was one of the most nutritious of the foods available in spring. And with luck perhaps they would find a squirrel. The spring diet was mostly grasses, roots, nuts. Meat would come later, but they could always hope for carrion of an old animal who had not made it through the winter. Even as the grizzly led the pup back to the den, she swung her head constantly to sniff, scanning for the distinctive smell of rotting flesh.

The grizzly had found a new den for spring and summer, one of the loveliest ever. It was in a thicket of alders on the river near a back eddy that would soon be busy with trout. Just outside the den's entrance, glacier lilies nodded their pale yellow heads. The steep bank down to the river was stippled with wild blue irises.

By the time they entered the den, Faolan was asleep. But he never slept so soundly that he couldn't nurse. The grizzly sat upright with her legs stuck straight out in front of her. While Faolan nursed, she watched the lavender twilight fall softly on the land. The river reflected the clouds on its glassy surface. It was different from the stormy night Faolan had arrived. She looked down at the pup, who was drunk with milk now.

She wondered about him more and more. The splayed paw was not that odd, but the faint tracery of swirling lines on the pad intrigued her. The swirls were so dim, but there was something almost hypnotic about the pattern of lines. What did it mean? Where had Faolan come from? Why had the river given him up to her? Was he lonely? Wolves were pack animals. Bears solitary. How could she be not just a mother but an entire pack to this wolf? "Urskadamus!" she muttered quietly.

The grizzly wondered all sorts of things. She knew wolves could not sit up like bears. So they must nurse their young in a very different way, perhaps lying down. But she was always worried about rolling over and crushing Faolan accidentally. He was so small and she so huge. And wolves could not stand up on their hind legs, let alone sit up. This seemed especially unfortunate. She saw so much standing up. She learned so much. It troubled her that Faolan could not do this. Would it, she wondered, be possible to teach a wolf to stand up and walk just a bit on his hind legs? She might try it. She looked down at him again and gave him a cuddle and a nuzzle. She loved him so. It was very odd, she knew. Other bears would look at her suspiciously. But she didn't care. She simply didn't care.

Faolan squirmed a bit and settled deeper down into his milk-laced sleep. He had grown accustomed to the percussive sounds of the grizzly's innards — the windy drafts of her gut as she digested, the bellowing inhalations and exhalations of her breathing, but most of all, the epic thumpings of her heart, that huge majestic heart. The sound wove through Faolan while he slept like a song for his milk dreams. The grizzly was no longer simply the Milk Giver in his mind, but Thunderheart.

CHAPTER FIVE

DEN LESSONS

IT WAS DURING THE FIRST SLIVER
of dawn that Thunderheart unceremoniously dumped
Faolan from her lap and gave him a gentle butt with her
nose on his muzzle. "Watch me!"

She left the den and he followed her down the banks
of the river to the rock slab that slid into the water. It was
his first fishing lesson. The trout at this time of the moon's
cycle would begin schooling in the back eddy by the rock.
Fishing took patience, and Thunderheart knew that wolf
pups, like bear cubs, were short on patience — especially
Faolan. But he was a quick learner. She hoped he was
ready for the very practical lesson of fishing. He just had
to fatten up. She worried incessantly about what she perceived as his smallness.

Fishing of course would be easier in the fall when the

salmon began their run up the river. Then all one had to do was wade on the upstream side of a small waterfall and catch the salmon as they flipped themselves toward their spawning grounds. Dumb with their urge to mate, they were easy prey. But trout were different. Free of any compulsion to spawn at this time of year and certainly having no obsessions about swimming upstream, trout were a challenge. No matter, Faolan must learn. He had to grow fatter, bigger.

The grizzly waited and peered into the amber water, scanning for the first flicker of a trout. She felt Faolan growing restless, and she knew he could not remain still much longer. But the fish didn't come. The pup whined a bit and wagged his head in the direction of a nearby cluster of sedges. She grunted her permission. Now she would have to keep one eye on the pup and one on the fish.

He was happy, though. The sedges provided an endless opportunity for nosing about for grubs and beetles and ladybugs, a favorite of bears and now a favorite of Faolan. He found a nest and was soon yipping with delight.

Faolan raised his muzzle, which was speckled with red dots. At the same moment Thunderheart glimpsed the flash of a trout. There was a loud *plash* as she smacked her forepaw into the river, grabbed the trout, and slapped it on the rock. Blood spurted into the air, the droplets caught in dazzling shards of light from the sun on the horizon.

Faolan froze. He smelled . . . blood. His eyes fixed on the spinning drops glittering madly in the morning light. His heart raced, he felt a quickness in his mouth. His tongue went suddenly wet. He was stunned by a new hunger aroused deep within him, and with an overwhelming admiration for Thunderheart. He shook his head fiercely to rid himself of the annoying ladybugs and meekly walked over to her.

Faolan lowered his head and then his entire body, flattening his ears as he flashed the whites of his eyes. Thunderheart softly woofed at him. "What are you doing?" she asked. Faolan had never appeared more wolfish, and yet she instinctively knew that he was showing her respect. But where had he learned this?

She knew the answer. Blood. With the claw-ripped body of the fish, she had awakened Faolan's blood passion. It was the same with cubs, but never had any of her cubs behaved in quite this way. They scrambled and tussled, trying to get in for the first nip of fresh meat, shoving and pushing rudely in their clamor to try this new taste. Faolan, however, was approaching her on his belly. *As if I am Ursus and no mere mother bear!*

She ripped the trout in two and dropped it in front of Faolan. But he hesitated and looked up at her with almost pleading eyes. She could see the saliva dripping from his mouth, but still he hesitated. She pushed the fish even closer to him. But Faolan only flattened himself farther and began to make small squeaking sounds. Thunderheart studied him carefully. She noticed that he stole a quick glance at the fish and then at her. Suddenly, it burst upon her: *I should eat first!*

But how, she wondered, *will he survive if he allows others to eat first?* Was this something wolves did? Pack behavior? *But he has to eat! He cannot give way to others, he will be eaten!* Her mind roiled with confusion.

She was rearing a wolf but knew only the way of bears.

Faolan remained flattened on his belly, stealing a glance at her sometimes, but mostly rolling his eyes back as if he dared not even look at her. Finally, she gave up and bit off the tail of the fish, making sure to leave the meatiest part for the pup.

Immediately, he pounced on what remained.

From that moment on, she never had a more ardent student of fishing. By mid-morning, Faolan was following Thunderheart into the river to swim behind her as they examined every cranny for schooling trout. The splayed paw served him well, and this, for Thunderheart, was perhaps the most rewarding aspect of the whole endeavor. Faolan became skillful at slapping and scooping with that odd front paw.

By mid-afternoon both Faolan and Thunderheart were stuffed with fish. They lay on a sunny bank and traced the path of clouds across the sky. Thunderheart grunted and raised one paw to point out a cloud that looked just like the trout they had been catching. Faolan yipped with glee and immediately began scanning the cloudscape for another picture. Suddenly, he jumped up in great excitement and began to beat his tail against the ground. Two towering clouds had silently collided, a hump bulging from one cloud near the top. Around that hump shoulders rose. Faolan yipped and Thunderheart sat up, too. Above the hump a smaller dark cloud was settling. Faolan could not contain his joy. "It's us! It's us! I ride you in the sky!"

And with that announcement, Faolan flung himself onto Thunderheart's back. The huge bear roared with delight, and the ground shook as they bounded off together, with Faolan perched on top of her.

CHAPTER SIX

BLOOD LESSON

THEY HAD NOT GONE FAR WHEN Thunderheart felt Faolan grow suddenly tense. She saw immediately what caught his attention. In a clearing, a mother grizzly and two cubs were making their way to the river to fish. The grizzly mother and cubs spotted them and froze in their tracks. Faolan tumbled from Thunderheart's back and scurried behind her, trying to hide. He nudged up against her hind leg, pressing into her fur. The mother and cubs approached cautiously. Faolan peered out, and the cubs both made chuffing sounds. They were laughing at him and he knew it! Their mother simply stared, dumbfounded. Thunderheart could feel Faolan shivering.

He knows he's different! It was bound to happen. Her first instinct was to shield him, prevent the bears from staring. But the more the mother stared and the more the little cubs chuffed — one was chuffing so hard it was rolling on the ground with glee at this odd sight — the more determined Thunderheart was not to shield Faolan. She moved her legs so that Faolan was exposed, and shuddered when she realized how tiny he was in comparison to the cubs.

Faolan made a mournful cry and looked up at Thunderheart. If she could have, she would have willed him to be twice his size. But she stood still as a rock. Not a sign, not a sound passed between them. All she could think of was that night she had dragged him from the river, that spark of life, nearly quenched yet still flickering. That fierceness!

Faolan caught something in her eyes. Slowly, he turned his head to the cubs, who were now convulsed with chuffing in the tall grass. In a split second, the pup's body transformed. His shivering stopped. He lifted his head high and began to walk forward with a regal bearing, his tail raised and his ears alert. The cubs' mother bristled with fear. She reached out and swatted the cub nearest to her. He yelped, and then his sister gave a gasp as she looked up from her tumbling and spotted Faolan.

The bear family regarded the pup with confusion now. How could something so small do this to them? Thunderheart herself was baffled. Faolan had not grown a speck bigger and yet somehow he appeared dominant. For one moment she had observed the pup caught between two worlds — one of which he had never seen. It was as if Faolan had joined something very important and very old, as if he were surrounded by the spirit of an invisible pack.

Then his tail began to waver just slightly and droop, and Thunderheart trotted over to him, grunted the command to follow, while reinforcing it with a light tap to his shoulder.

The mother grizzly blinked. Who was this strange creature who looked like a wolf, but now was behaving like a bear cub?

In truth, all the animals were confused, including Faolan. As he trotted behind Thunderheart, one thought ran through his head: *I am different. I am different. I am different.*

On their way back to the den, they passed a small inlet from the river where they had fished. The water was still, undisturbed by current. Faolan paused and peered down at the gleaming surface. Thunderheart came up beside him, wondering if he had found more fish. Both their reflections quivered on the surface of the dark water. *I look nothing like her, nothing like any animal I have seen. Why are my eyes so green? Why is my face so narrow?*

Thunderheart's face is huge, wider than my chest. Her fur is
so thick and dark. My fur is too bright.

They returned to the den. Out of habit, Faolan clamped
on to Thunderheart's teat. As he nursed he looked gravely
into her eyes, and she saw a question in the deep green
pools of light. *Why am I not like you?* She growled softly
and licked his nose in answer.

Love, she thought, *love is all that matters.* But she
did not say these words aloud. Bears, being solitary creatures, had great reserve and did not often give voice to
their most powerful feelings. It was as if to utter such
thoughts aloud was to diminish them. But she looked into
Faolan's eyes, and he, who had learned the ways of the
bears, met her gaze. Engulfed in the deep amber light of
Thunderheart's eyes, the wolf understood that he was
different. And he knew he was loved, as if he were her
own cub.

He would not be able to nurse much longer, for
Thunderheart sensed that her milk was drying up. She
was happy that they had been successful with the fish,
but knew that she must now teach him to go after the
real meat, the red meat. This might be easier than she

had thought, for it was Faolan who had first sensed the mother grizzly and her cubs. He must have picked up their scent. And if so, he had done it faster than she had. A good thing for hunting red meat.

They both slept through the rising heat of the day and into the late afternoon.

Thunderheart thought she smelled the bear coming. But she could not move. Her limbs felt heavy. It was as if she had sunk into cold sleep. This is not winter, *she told herself.* I must move. My cubs . . . my cubs. Yet if it is cold sleep it is not mating time. So why should I have scent marked? Why am I so confused? Was there time to scent mark? *She could hardly lift her head, let alone rise to her full height and mark the trees near the den. A torrent of blood slashed the perfect blue of the sky as the great male grizzly ripped open the back of her cub to its bone. Thunderheart rose up, roared, and charged the male. She tore at his arm. A deep gash. He screeched in pain and ran off. But was it a mortal injury? She feared not. He would be back. . . . He would be back. . . .*

Thunderheart woke up from the horrific dream with a violent shake that spilled the wolf pup from the lap.

"Urskadamus!" she muttered. Faolan blinked at her in alarm. He pulled back his lips in a grimace of fear, the hackles on the back of his neck rising as he tucked his tail between his hind legs. The grizzly huffed nervously. The time was coming when she knew the males would be feeling the urge for her company. If she could scent mark before she was fertile and before such a male came into her territory, it would be good.

She knew that wolves scent marked as well. This might truly confuse other bears. She had no inclination to mate. Faolan was her last cub, and she was determined to do the best possible for him. No male was going to harm him or run him off.

But could he learn to stand up and walk, even run like a bear? He could jump quite high when he wanted a ride on her hump. He could almost reach her shoulder and she knew he could scent mark. He had certainly urinated in the area around the den, but more scent marking was needed; the other special kind that she had sometimes caught wind of when she passed wolf territory.

This was a practical lesson. Unlike the notion of love which could not be expressed in words, this one could be spoken, with very clear actions to accompany the words. Faolan's language skills had grown. Thunderheart had heard wolves and owls speak on occasion and at the time thought the words were so different from her own, but they weren't at all. It was merely the tones, the register in which they were uttered that seemed strange. She sometimes thought of it as water. The sound of water in a fast-running brook differs from the clamor of a falls or the trickle of a stream in the dry season. But it was all water. One just had to listen.

Faolan's voice was shallower, not as deep as her own. Owls' tones varied widely. Some were almost hollow, others more sonorous, and a few screechy. None of the owls' voices were remotely like that of a bear, and yet the words were almost identical. Nevertheless, Faolan was beginning to sound slightly bearish when he spoke. He was acquiring some of the rough, back-of-the-throat sounds that were common to the grizzlies.

And as soon as they were out of the den, Faolan scampered toward the riverbank. Thunderheart gave him a low snarl and a firm head butt to his flanks that spun Faolan around in the direction that she wanted him to follow. "This way!"

She swung her head toward a large white pine, then

rose up halfway on her hind legs and began rubbing her back against the tree. There was a harsh scratching sound. She was leaving a scent, but it was not the odor of a female, fertile and receptive to mating. Faolan must leave a scent as well, his own scent.

Thunderheart stared at him hard. She sensed that Faolan must do this scenting with his hindquarters. She lowered herself now and sprawled on the ground and woofed softly for him to come over as she often did when they tussled. He immediately clambered onto her back. A strong odor rose through the thick fur from the stimulated scent glands beneath her skin.

"What's that?"

"My scent."

Faolan had smelled that scent before when he had ridden on her, but now it was stronger, almost overpowering, and very different from the thick sweet smell of the milk. It was a strong signal. A defensive message that this den and everything around it from the white spruce to the riverbank and up to the grove of alders belonged to Thunderheart, and to him, her pup. It triggered something in Faolan. "I can do that!"

He sank into the thick, odiferous fur and nuzzled her neck, licking the inside of her ear and then tumbling off to run to the nearest tree. Thunderheart watched him as he backed his hindquarters against it and lowered his tail. *He is quick!* Thunderheart thought. She hadn't had to explain anything, really. He had immediately understood the urgency of this scent message. *What a remarkable young pup!*

A muscle at the top of Faolan's tail contracted as he began to rub against the trunk. He felt something release. Immediately, he began running about marking every tree, rock, and stump he could find. *Mine! Mine! Mine!* The thought coursed through his being. But this was only the beginning. As he marked, there were stirrings in other parts of his body. He began to scratch furiously at the ground. Another scent from between his toes was emitted, and the cry in his head, *Mine! Mine! Mine!*, changed to *Ours! Ours! Ours!* Something had unlocked deep in his wolf history.

But Thunderheart was the only other creature that he knew. He paused and looked at her once more. She stood by a tree that she was rubbing, not half crouched as before, but tall and majestic. She eyed him with the deep tawny light he loved so much, and yet now there was challenge in her eyes. She huffed and barked. "Come on, come on!"

Faolan cocked his head. He began to jump up for a ride on her hump, but each time she moved to another tree before he could catch her, waving her arms and batting the branches above her.

Some bright green leaves caught the last of the setting sun's light as they fluttered down. He leaped up to catch a leaf before it hit the ground. Thunderheart made a low amiable grunt and then shook the tree again. Faolan leaped again. They played this game for a while. Each time Faolan jumped a bit higher.

Then Thunderheart turned from the tree and continued walking, still on her hind legs. She looked back to see Faolan following, but on all fours. She stopped abruptly, faced him, and lowered herself down briefly. Next, she rose up, waving her arms as she had when she had encouraged him to jump at the tree. "Two legs!" she commanded.

Faolan stood very still. It was almost as if she could see his mind turning over what she had just proposed. He rose up on his hind legs. Thunderheart watched, hardly daring to breathe. Tentatively, Faolan took a step toward her.

Thunderheart grunted happily and lowered herself to lick Faolan under his chin, making soft chuffing sounds.

She spotted a low shrub with some plump berries and broke off a branch. Then, raising herself up again on her hind legs, she waved the branch in front of Faolan. She knew he loved these berries. Instantly, he was on his hind legs walking. This time he took four steps! Thunderheart was thrilled.

He was learning and she was delighted with herself for teaching him. Cubs knew how to do this almost from the start. It was natural for them. But it wasn't natural for Faolan. She was beginning to realize that Faolan was not just an exceptional pup, but an extraordinary creature.

By the time darkness fell, Faolan was walking on his hind legs almost as well as a cub. And, on that brink of time between the last drop of daylight and the first purple darkness, Faolan learned his best lesson. He caught a flash of white as an ermine scuttled into a burrow on the far side of a tall shrub, something he would have never seen had he not been upright. He sprang in one arcing leap across the shrub and landed on all fours, madly digging. The splayed front paw had grown stronger since he had been forced to use it. He never thought twice about it now.

Thunderheart trotted up behind him as a storm of dirt spun through the air. Suddenly, a furry dart shot from the nest. Faolan staggered backward and tumbled heels over tail as something lunged onto his back. Sharp digging claws. He leaped up into the air and twisted himself, trying to get rid of the horrid attacker. It was much smaller than he was, not much bigger than a squirrel, but it was strong. Faolan yelped as the sharp claws and teeth dug deeper. Thunderheart roared. She could not risk swatting the ermine from his back without injuring Faolan. They fought fiercely: The pup had just torn apart her nest and her young kits quivered in fear. If the ermine got near Faolan's neck and the vital life-pumping artery, he would be finished.

Thunderheart was frantic. She could see that Faolan was weakening already, losing energy. This was his first real blood battle. Thunderheart tried to false charge, but the ermine paid no attention. Faolan sank to his knees, rose up again, and this time streaked toward the riverbank. In one flying leap, he plunged into the water. Thunderheart plunged in after him. She watched his head break through the surface. Red streaks coursed down the back of his neck, but on the opposite side of the river she saw the ermine slink up the steep muddy bank.

In the den that night as leaves outside rustled with warm summer breezes, Thunderheart licked Faolan's wounds. They were not as deep as she had feared. They would heal, but she sensed a new restlessness in the pup. He did not nurse. He was done with milk. He wanted blood.

CHAPTER SEVEN

THE GOLDEN EYES
OF THUNDERHEART

THE LESSONS CONTINUED THROUGH the summer. Faolan loved learning. He became more and more proficient at rearing up, and he could walk for extended distances upright. His hind legs were becoming very powerful, and because they were more flexible than a bear's, he could jump very high. He took a puppyish delight in showing off his leaping skills.

There was an immense spruce tree near the den, the lowest limbs of which were almost as high as Thunderheart's shoulders when she stood. Nearly every afternoon they went to this tree. Faolan was determined to reach that limb by springing up on his hind legs.

"Watch me! Watch me!" he yapped. Each day he got closer. "Watch me, Thunderheart! You're not paying attention!" he'd scold. "I'm almost there!"

And then one day he made it. He found himself draped over the limb above the one he had aimed for. He was stunned. "Urskadamus!" he yelped. The curse startled Thunderheart.

"Where did you learn that?" she roared.

"From you!"

She chuffed heartily.

"Don't laugh at me! I'm stuck!"

"You jumped too high. You weren't paying attention!" she added slyly.

"How do I get down?"

"I don't know. I've never been stuck that high in a tree," she replied.

Faolan gave a plangent little yelp.

"No whining!" She turned her back and walked away as if she didn't have a care in the world.

Faolan stared at her broad back in dismay. "You're leaving me like this?"

"You'll figure it out," she said without turning around. "You're the smartest youngster I know."

A few seconds later she heard a soft thud as Faolan dropped to the ground.

He was soon at her side, wagging his tail. "I did it!"

"I knew you would!" She turned her head and gave him a soft bump with her muzzle.

All summer long the pup grew, although to Thunderheart he still seemed small compared to a bear cub. For a wolf pup, however, Faolan was large and very strong. He had abilities that ordinary wolves simply did not possess. He was a wolf without a pack, which made him fiercely independent. And since he had acquired the taste for meat, he had become proficient at hunting down the four-footed animals, the occasional ptarmigan, and other ground-nesting birds. Swifter on his feet than Thunderheart and with a keenness for strategy, he had managed to chase an injured caribou into a narrow defile and trap him. When Thunderheart arrived, she brought the animal down with a single blow. This strategy worked so well that the two had done it several times since that first occasion.

"I love caribou," Faolan said one day after they'd brought down another one. "Where do they come from?"

"Different places at different times. In the spring they come down from the Outermost."

"The Outermost?"

"North of here. The taste of the caribou from the Outermost in the spring is the best."

"How do you get there?"

Thunderheart pointed to the North Star. "In the early spring, when the Great Bear constellation rises, you follow the last claw in the foot that points to the North Star. The Outermost is in between that claw and the North Star. I once had a den there. Someday . . ."

"Someday what?" Faolan asked. Thunderheart looked troubled and didn't answer. "Someday we'll go back?"

"Perhaps. But I am not sure if it is good for your kind."

"My kind?" Faolan felt his heart race. "But the Outermost, it is good for your kind? If it's good for your kind, it's good for my kind."

"Never mind, never mind. Eat up." She was about to say more, but Faolan interrupted.

"I know, I know," Faolan said wearily. "I must grow fat for winter."

"Yes, eat that liver." She yanked out the bloody organ and tossed it to him.

He obediently began eating, but his mind turned over what Thunderheart had said. *I am not sure if it is good for your kind*. He didn't like the way it sounded and didn't want to hear it again, out loud or in his mind. He would simply seal up his ears.

Together the grizzly and the wolf pup would often hunt late into the summer evenings until the stars broke out. Faolan liked to sleep near the opening of the den, where he could see the stars and hear the star stories that Thunderheart told him. By now the words and the hidden language of bears beneath the words had become completely transparent to Faolan.

Thunderheart would point her paw toward the sky and trace the star picture of the Great Bear constellation with her longest claw. "He leads the way to Ursulana," she whispered. It was to Ursulana, the bear heaven, where Thunderheart was sure her cub's spirit had traveled.

Every star seemed to have a story, and every animal a constellation. Faolan was impressed that Thunderheart knew so many. She pointed to the west of the Star Bear to the Wolf constellation. "It's disappearing now in the middle of summer. It shines the brightest and rises the highest in spring, but look, there are the Great Claws."

Faolan blinked as a clawlike figure began to creep up over the purple horizon. "It's late, but it stays the longest, arriving in early winter and staying through summer. If you go to the banks of Hoolemere, you can see the young owls of the Great Ga'Hoole Tree practicing their navigation exercises by tracing it. The owls call the Great Claws the Golden Talons."

"Hoolemere? Great — what do you call it — Tree? Navigation?" Faolan asked. He was completely bewildered.

Thunderheart made a snuffling sound, which was the way she laughed sometimes. "You're young and you haven't seen much! Hoolemere is a vast sea, and there is a group of owls who live on an island in a huge tree in the middle of that sea. These owls are called the Guardians of Ga'Hoole. They are very intelligent owls."

"You mean smart?" Faolan asked.

"Yes, very smart."

"As smart as you?"

"Oh, much smarter! They can find their way to many places just by looking at the stars and how they move. That is what navigation is — finding one's way by the stars."

"But you told me about the star to the north. You find your way by it."

"That's easy. That star never moves. It only sits high in the sky. It's my only guide. But the owls use all the stars — the whole sky."

"That's probably because they fly and know it better."

Thunderheart gave the pup a little squeeze. What a smart little wolf he was!

Faolan yawned and said sleepily, "Someday maybe I'll go to the banks of Hoolemere and maybe even swim to the island. Such a funny word, 'Hoole.' What does it mean?"

"Well," Thunderheart sighed, "some say that it is actually a wolf word and that it is their word for 'owl.'" But by this time Faolan was fast asleep in her arms.

With the waning days of summer, Thunderheart had but one thought: *Eat!* Eat all one could for the winter! The cold sleep was coming and the two of them must have enough fat. But beyond her overwhelming obsession about Faolan's size and the question of fat, there was another more elusive fear — that of the cold sleep itself. Soon she would have to find a winter den farther away from the river. She was not sure if wolves went into their dens and slept for endless days. How would she know? She had slumbered through every winter of her life. She knew nothing of the winter world and what other animals did. How would she explain this to Faolan? She knew that she changed during this sleep. She grew thinner and if she did rouse herself, her mind was foggy. If she slept and he didn't, how would she protect him? Perhaps she should warn him. But not right now.

Right now, the salmon were swimming up the river to their spawning ground. Thunderheart and Faolan had waded out to the shallows on the upstream side of a small rapid where scores of salmon were heaving themselves forward. Thunderheart scooped them from the water or caught them on the fly.

It was the easiest fishing Faolan had ever done. He paused for a moment and looked at Thunderheart. Facing west, the setting sun turned her eyes gold. He felt a sudden surge of affection sweep through him as he realized how different they were. He had put out of his mind that day months before when they had seen the grizzly mother with the two cubs. He had since then refused to allow such thoughts to enter his mind. Except he now remembered a few days earlier when they had brought down a caribou, and Thunderheart had first mentioned the Outermost and how it might not be a good place for his "kind."

Thunderheart had mentioned wolves a few times, but

Faolan had never seen any, except for the Star Wolf in the sky. So the notion of a real wolf was vague. The thought of wolves did not trouble him, for when he looked into the golden eyes of Thunderheart, he felt his world was complete. Those eyes offered a universe. He needed nothing else.

That evening was their last night in the river den. The next morning, well before dawn, they began their trek to find a winter den in the higher elevations of the Beyond. Thunderheart was particular about her winter den. Most grizzlies dug out dens under large tree roots. But the trees were few in this part of the Beyond, and what trees there were grew at lower elevations. If a bear went above the sparse tree line, there were good natural rock caves to be found, even tunnels in the lava beds. But most important, the snow came earlier in the high country, insulating the den for a longer period of time.

By mid-morning, they had crossed the broad flat meadow, and Thunderheart was pushing her bulk through the low-growing bracken and nettles at the base of a long slope. They were almost above the tree line. The air was thinner and the going harder. Thunderheart's breath came in labored bellowing huffs, but she marveled at

Faolan, who never seemed to tire. His chest had broadened, she noticed, and she suspected it might have been because of his jumping, which he loved to practice. It was hard to imagine that a brief four months before he had been a whiny little pup dramatically flinging himself onto the dirt and waving his splayed paw in the air. Now he scampered ahead. He had already pounced on a marmot and made quick work of him. His muzzle was still covered in blood.

Thunderheart had insisted that Faolan consume the liver entirely himself, for she knew that it was rich and would give him fat. She would never cease worrying about his size. And she was not ready yet to warn him about how she changed during the cold sleep. *Not yet . . . not yet*, she told herself.

The days had shortened considerably, and by late afternoon, as the long shafts of the setting sun angled across the short grass of the slope, Thunderheart found what she thought might be a suitable winter den. It was near a rock where they had commenced digging. Thunderheart's paws were much larger than Faolan's, but Faolan anchored himself firmly by the four toes of his back paws and dug furiously with his five-toed front paws. The fifth toe was somewhat smaller, and Thunderheart had wondered once what such a small claw could accomplish. It turned out to be perfect for digging.

The bear and the wolf had not been working long before both of them struck something hard. Faolan looked up in surprise and paused, but Thunderheart grew excited. She had heard that sound before! It was a hollow *kah-kah* noise. In another minute, she grunted in delight. They had uncovered a lava bed with a natural tunnel that had been made from the flow of an inactive volcano to the north and west. Off the first tunnel, there was an elevated section that would trap heat and provide good drainage if there were any leaks from above.

"This is perfect," she said, looking around. "Just perfect."

"Perfect for winter?" Faolan asked, for he had the feeling Thunderheart was referring to something else.

The grizzly looked at him now. Her gaze was very serious. "I must explain something to you, pup."

Faolan felt a dread stir deep within him. *Please don't talk about wolves again. Not wolves!*

"I am not sure what wolves do, but bears sleep through the winter. Our hearts grow slower and beat but a few times when there were many beats before."

"Mine, too! Mine, too!" Faolan said. Although he could feel his heart racing.

"No, Faolan, yours doesn't."

"I'm just like you, Thunderheart."

"No, you're different. I sense you are not going to sleep as deeply as I do."

"I'll try. I promise!"

"You can try all you want. But that doesn't matter. You will most likely grow bored here." She glanced around at the tunnel.

"Oh, no! No, I won't! I love to watch you sleep."

Thunderheart lifted a paw to silence him.

"Don't interrupt. You're big now. You will get hungry. All I am saying is that if you grow hungry and bored, you have my permission to go out. Snow rabbits are plentiful here. They don't sleep. I am sure of that."

Faolan was suddenly alarmed. "Are you saying I am like a snow rabbit? Are you telling me to go play with a snow rabbit?" His voice seethed with indignation.

"Faolan!" Thunderheart roared, and the lava rock walls of the tunnel shivered. "Don't act stupid. I'm telling you to go out and kill the rabbit, eat it. Not play with it!"

"Oh!" said Faolan meekly.

CHAPTER EIGHT

THE WINTER DEN

IT WAS NOT LONG AFTER THE wolf and the grizzly moved into the winter den that Thunderheart began the cold sleep. In the beginning, it was just short snoozes and she often told Faolan to go out and scour the slope for rabbits and marmots. She wanted to get him used to going out alone. He would always bring some meat back for Thunderheart in his gut. He had learned through some primal instinct that the large chunks of meat that lodged in his first stomach could be regurgitated in steaming piles on the floor of the den for Thunderheart. The first time he did this, she roused herself from the thick blanket of sleep in which she was folded, but it became more and more difficult to wake her after the first heavy snowfall. Thunderheart slept so deeply that, just as she had explained to Faolan, her immense heart began to beat slower and more quietly. It was as if a deep hush had fallen upon her and she sank deeper and deeper into an insensate sleep.

Faolan did not like the quiet. It unsettled him. The sound of that great heart was his first memory. So it was not simply boredom that drove him from the den, but the silence. Despite Thunderheart's immense size, she seemed in her stillness a shadow of her summer self. Faolan could not understand how she slept so much. And, as the rhythms of Thunderheart's body slowed, it seemed that those of Faolan's accelerated.

The deeper the snow outside, the better for Faolan. He loved bounding through the drifts and making huge powdery explosions. Down on the flats of the meadow, the wind had pounded the snow into a great hard surface, and he enjoyed skidding and coasting games. He had become expert at tracking the big snow hares and found their meat delectable.

He loved everything about winter — the strange green sky as twilight descended, then the deep purple dark of the night and the glittering jewel star that hung in the north and never moved, but guided him back to the den. The ice-spangled bracken poking through the drifts were as luminous as the constellations that floated in the dome of the night. One night soon after the first snowfall, he had spied in the distance a spectacular sight. It was the waterfall they had passed on their way to the winter den. But now the cascades were frozen in the air, suspended like silver flames caught in a wintry eternity.

Each day was shorter as the earth tipped farther away from the sun. But the nights were longer. Once he thought he heard something new in the night — a long melodious howl that inscribed itself in the blackness like an unfurling banner of song. It stirred him profoundly. It was new to him, yet oddly familiar. He felt compelled to howl in return. It was amazing to him that he understood perfectly the message embedded in the howl: *I am here, here with my mate. Our sister and brothers have returned. In one more moon, when the mating times come, we shall move.*

Faolan understood the message, but there were strange pieces of it that made no sense. What was a sister? A brother?

Each night for the next cycle of the moon, he went out to hear the wolves. He understood more and more, but despite his growing curiosity, he did not dare travel closer. For there was a warning woven into the message: *This is our territory. Do not trespass.* The warning was as clear as any scent mark. By the end of the moon's cycle, the howling had finished. The wolves had left as they promised.

For the first time, Faolan felt a bit lonely. He returned to the den after the first songless night and looked at Thunderheart. *How long will she sleep?* he wondered. She no longer slept sitting up, but instead lay on her side. He curled up next to her and listened to the slow beating of her heart. *So slow, so slow,* he thought. And yet still he found profound comfort in its languid rhythm.

There came a day when the earth began to tilt toward the sun. The darkness near the entrance of the den seemed thinner, and Faolan even detected a slight quickening in the beating of the grizzly's heart. *Perhaps this lonely time is coming to an end,* he thought.

Faolan still made his forays out to hunt for the tasty snow hares and marmots. One day as the morning lengthened, he went farther from the den than he had in a long time. The day had turned very warm and great slabs of ice began to slide down the inclines, peeling back the slope until dun-colored grasses began to poke through. It was a great day for hunting and he ignored the storm clouds gathering in the west on the horizon.

Meanwhile, back in the den Thunderheart began to stir. It was much too early for her to leave the cold sleep, but she felt an absence, a void in the den that pushed her from her slumber.

It was a dangerous time for a bear to be out. Winter had not made its last mark. Bears were weak, their reflexes slow despite their hunger, which was always overwhelming at the end of the cold sleep. If a bear ventured out, the first danger, aside from sudden changes in the weather, was encountering another bear who was just as hungry. Territorial markings had not been made. Tempers raged and bear fights were inevitable. Thunderheart knew this, even in her sleep-drugged state. And although she was not extremely hungry, she was terrified when she discovered that Faolan had gone. In her confusion, she forgot that she had expressly given Faolan permission to leave the den and go out to hunt.

Thunderheart was determined to find him. But when she crawled out of the den, she gasped. A sudden blizzard had torn in from the west, turning the world white. Tracks were covered instantly, and when she looked up, she could not even see a dim smear of the North Star's light. Still, she had to go out. She had to find the pup. She knew Faolan's scent. The blizzard could not cover it completely. If he had found prey he might have marked a small hunting ground. She was desperate to find him. Desperate and confused.

With the blizzard blowing so ferociously it was difficult to discern what time of day or night it was. The entire world had dissolved into an impenetrable whiteness. But Faolan made his way back to the den. He was shocked to find it empty. Had Thunderheart gone deeper into the tunnels when the blizzard started? He explored briefly but he knew her scent, and there was no sign of her. He began to pace. He tried to imagine what might have happened to her or where she could have gone. He had picked up no scent on his own journey back to the den. It seemed as if she had simply vanished. *She wouldn't have left me. . . . No, never. She would never just leave me.* The very thought sent a tremor through Faolan until the hackles on his neck and every guard hair on his back stood straight up. It reminded him of something, something that had happened long, long ago that he couldn't quite remember. She would come back, he reasoned. She had to!

He waited all that night and into the next day. He paid no heed to the grumbles of his empty stomach. Food meant nothing to him. There was only one thing he wanted: Thunderheart. The den was too quiet. The beat of her enormous heart, even in its slow winter rhythms, was gone. He could not live without the sound. It was all he knew, all he had ever known. He stepped out of the den into the rage of the blizzard and began howling. Howling for the great grizzly. Howling for all he had ever known and loved.

Then as he howled, an odd tremor rose through the depths of the snow, from the frozen land beneath it, from the very center of the earth. The tremblings were like faint quivers, but Faolan pressed his splayed front paw deep and these tremulous shakings became quite distinct. And then more incredibly powerful. For a moment, it felt as if the entire snowfield had shifted under his paws, and in the distance, he saw the frozen waterfall crack and suddenly gush to life.

But in that second he thought of death. And he knew with an overpowering certainty that something terrible was happening to his beloved Thunderheart.

CHAPTER NINE

A DIM MEMORY

ON THE FAR EDGE OF THE BEYOND, the she-wolf Morag had been absorbed into a new pack. She had found a new mate and given birth to a healthy litter of pups. No one knew her history, and in fact, she herself had all but forgotten it. The minute the Obea had walked away with that pup in her mouth to deliver it to a *tummfraw*, the place for abandonment of malformed pups, Morag began to build up barriers deep within her. These barriers functioned like a kind of invisible scar tissue to toughen her so that she could go on, survive. Such was the way with wolf mothers who had endured the special anguish of losing a *malcadh* pup to an Obea. They quickly forgot. In the wake of forgetting, there was for a time a darkness deep within them where that pup had grown inside their bodies. But it soon faded until it became merely a gray shadow of which they were hardly aware. They had to be this way if they were going to go on, find another mate, and bear more pups.

Morag was now consumed with a rambunctious trio of red-furred pups. At nearly a moon cycle old, they were busy exploring the whelping den with their milk teeth. They were becoming bolder as well, and began to scramble closer to the white light of the den opening. Morag's mate helped keep them back. Soon, when the pups were just a bit bigger, Morag and her mate would let them out regularly to explore under careful supervision. At that point, the pups would begin to eat meat. Then they would be weaned, and finally a den must be found near the rest of the packs that made up the MacDonegal clan.

Morag had decided that today she would leave her mate in charge and set out toward the heart of the MacDonegal territory to begin the search for an appropriate den. The weather was still blustery from the remnants of the storm that had blown in from the north, bringing heavy snows to the border between the Beyond and the Outermost. But here it was merely sloppy with rain and sleet. To the west, the sky was clearing and there was the promise of better weather.

Morag ambled along a creek bed. Since the earthquake, it was as if the territory had been entirely rearranged. Boulders that she had never seen before had tumbled from mountains and blocked up several parts of the creek, causing small pools to form. It was no longer a simple task to follow the creek to the middle of the MacDonegal territory. After several hours of travel, Morag found that she had swung far out of MacDonegal territory and skirted closer to the river that ran into the Outermost.

It was not, however, a tumbled boulder that caught her attention, but a small creek stone polished to a gleaming black finish by the water. She had just set her front paws in a shallow pool when she spotted it. It sparkled like a dark moon in the water and when she looked closely, she saw a pattern of swirling lines. Like eddies in the creek, the lines spiraled around and around. There was something vaguely hypnotic about the spinning design. But more than hypnotic, it kindled a dim memory in Morag. It was disturbing. She turned stiff-legged in the stream with her tail pointing straight out and howled her alarm.

But instead of a response from other wolves, a jagged sound cut the air. *Kra! Kra!* It was the call of a raven announcing the discovery of a carcass. This was not just an announcement, but also a summons for help. Without the ripping teeth of wolves, it was impossible for ravens to penetrate the thick hide of a large animal. Usually, this sound would have excited Morag. But not on this day. If she had been in the company of her pups, the raven's call would have offered a lesson. But now she only shrank from the sound.

As she stood in the creek her eyes were drawn back to the swirl of lines on the polished rock. *What is this? What is it that so haunts me?*

The raven's *kra kra* again laced the air. The spinning pattern and the *kras* mingled in the deep recesses of her memory. Haltingly, she took a few steps toward the other bank.

Almost as soon as Morag left the creek, she spotted two ravens circling a short distance ahead. In a clearing she saw the immense carcass of a grizzly. Her first thought was one of slight disbelief. Why would a grizzly come this far south at this time of year? It should still be winter-denning.

She swung her head toward the north and west, the far reaches of the Beyond in the low mountains, where the grizzlies frequently lived and denned. She knew from when she had traveled with the MacDuncan clan that it was always bad when a grizzly came out of its winter den too early.

Morag approached the carcass. If it had been in a fight, there were few wounds, at least not enough to help the ravens. She walked slowly around the body until she spotted a terrible head wound near the grizzly's ear, where the ravens had already torn away what flesh they could. The bear was on its side, and she could see bone protruding from its back. She stopped and peered at it.

The grizzly's back had been broken by an enormous force. Morag looked up. A short distance away was an immense boulder, smeared with blood. The earthquake, of course! The boulder had tumbled down from the ridge above. The bear must have been in its path. It wasn't a living animal that had ended this bear's life, but the spasms of the earth itself.

The two ravens perched on the bear's hip, clearly indicating that this was the site they expected Morag to rip open for their feast. The ravens were already intoxicated by the scent of blood. But Morag caught the thread of another scent. The scar tissue that had so subtly built up within her began to dissolve. The first shadows of darkness began to steal back in from that empty place she had so completely sealed off.

She became agitated and began nervously racing around the carcass, burrowing her nose into the bear's thick fur, first beneath its huge arm, then beneath its haunches. The ravens became raucous; soon they were confused. What was the wolf doing?

Morag circled back toward the grizzly's shoulders, where an immense hump rose like a mountain. But even without poking it with her muzzle, a familiar scent drifted from the dense fur. Morag's hackles rose and her eyes rolled. She knew this scent. The pup from the year before! From the time she had traveled to the far edge of the Beyond to find a birthing den away from her old pack. The pup the Obea had taken, the one with the splayed paw marked with the spiral print.

Every bit of that sad time rushed back to her: how she was forced to return with the Obea and the remaining pups, and was then cast out of the clan. For an entire moon cycle afterward, she would find the highest point of land each night and tip her head toward the sky, searching for the track of stars called the spirit trail that led to the Great Wolf, Lupus, and the Cave of Souls. She was waiting for *lochinmorrin*, when her unnamed pup with its splayed paw would begin to climb the spirit trail. Then she would know that his abandonment had ended in death, and he had found peace in the Cave of Souls. But *lochinmorrin* had never come. She had never seen the soft mist of his *lochin*, the soul of a departed wolf.

He had not died, but she had wiped him from her memory until this moment. She sat down on her haunches close to the carcass of the bear. She pressed her head into its flanks. This bear had cared for her pup. She would not rip into the grizzly's body. She would keep watch over it through the night. She would let no predator near. This would be like *lochinvyrr*, the ritual that wolves followed when they brought down an animal and it was dying. It was a demonstration of respect in which the killer acknowledged that the life he was taking was a worthy one. Although Morag had not brought down this bear, she felt it was her duty to acknowledge the grizzly as worthy, for she had reared a wolf pup as if it were her own cub. The *lochin* of this magnificent bear would follow that spirit trail of stars to its own Cave of Souls. It was all she could do for the bear who had become the Milk Giver for her own pup, and allowed it to survive.

PART
TWO
THE OUTERMOST

CHAPTER TEN

THE FROST FOREST

SOMETHING TERRIBLE HAD HAPPENED to Thunderheart, but what? It had been days since the earth had trembled, since the frozen waterfall had broken free of its chamber of ice. The landscape had drastically rearranged itself. There were huge gashes in the snowfield, immense boulders had appeared where there had never been any before. Some of these gashes were as deep as the mountains were tall. The day after the earthquake, Faolan had seen a moose suddenly vanish. There were no trees around, no cave. The moose was there one second and gone the next. Curious, Faolan had cautiously made his way to the spot where the moose had disappeared. He followed a seam that looked like no more than a dent in the snow, but then split wide just ahead where the moose had been standing. The animal had crashed through. Faolan could hear it now, baying deep in the earth. He stopped in his tracks, standing in the middle of a death trap. There was a maze of these snow-covered seams that disguised deep crevices where the earth had cracked. Had Thunderheart been swallowed by one? Faolan grew weak at the thought of her dying alone in the bottom of an icy crevice.

But for Faolan, there was one thought even worse than Thunderheart's death: abandonment. Could she have left him? Although he and Thunderheart sometimes talked about the night she had fetched him from the river, their conversation always stopped short. He never asked her why he had been left to drown. He had never dared to think that his wolf mother could have done this to him.

He decided it had been some terrible accident that had all worked out well. He had not been *abandoned*; he had been *found*. By Thunderheart.

But now the questions he had so successfully resisted seemed to ambush him. Had he, back when he was just a tiny newborn pup, been left to die? Had Thunderheart now left him because he wasn't her *kind*? The ugly word seared through his brain, but it reminded him of something.

That place, the Outermost! Thunderheart had spoken about the taste of the caribou from the Outermost being the best in the spring. She'd once had a den there. But when Faolan had said that someday they could go together, she had replied, "Perhaps. But I am not sure if it is good for your kind."

Of course! thought Faolan. *That must be where she has gone.* She hadn't abandoned him at all. She had gone to get caribou and she would bring it back.

Through the maze of snow seams he cautiously made his way back to the winter den. But when she had not returned in another few days and hunting became more precarious in the fractured snowfield, Faolan decided to head north, toward the Outermost, to find her. He did not care if it was good or not for his kind. He needed to be with Thunderheart. And he knew how to get there. All he had to do was follow the last claw in the foot of the Great Bear constellation, which pointed to the North Star. "The Outermost is in between." Those had been Thunderheart's exact words.

Faolan knew it would be a long trip. But he was determined. Along the way, he sought temporary shelters, although they never seemed as nice or as cozy as those he had shared with Thunderheart. How could they be? Despite the warming weather, they were cold places without the comfort of the sound of that great, drumming heart. Those rhythms had been as much a part of Faolan as the beating of his own heart.

Faolan had just roused himself from a short nap in a cave far to the north of Thunderheart's winter den. The cycle of one moon had passed since Thunderheart had disappeared. And although the weather was growing warmer, there were still patches of snow in the territory he entered. He was surprised to see that the trees were different here as well. There were hardly any broadleaved trees, but mostly the kind with green needles and the cones that Thunderheart loved to eat. Faolan wondered if he was getting close to the Outermost.

Since it was colder, the trees also kept their frost longer. So even now as he wove his way through the closely growing trees, their needles prickled with minuscule stars of frost, wrapping the woods in a dazzling radiance. Sometimes the trees thinned and for great stretches the land became almost entirely barren. The ground was covered with lichen, which Thunderheart had told him made for fat caribou. Perhaps this was a sign that he was drawing closer to the Outermost. He decided to push on.

A few nights, Faolan heard the howling of wolves, and at first he was excited. But the howls were as different from the ones he had heard in the Beyond as the trees were. They were not melodious in the least, and seemed oddly meaningless. More like crude snarls in the night. Indeed, if the howls reminded him of anything, it was of that cataclysmic moment when he had felt the earth move. He had thought perhaps the world had been possessed of the foaming-mouth disease that Thunderheart had warned him about. She had told him to beware of any animal with a foaming mouth. He must never hunt one, but stay as far as possible from such a creature, even if it was a tiny ground squirrel.

Although Faolan felt sure he was entering the Outermost, it was frustrating that he had not picked up the scent of any grizzly. He ached for that old summer den where the glacier lilies grew and the banks of the river were thick with irises. The gilded summer mornings he spent swimming and looking for trout now felt as fragile and fleeting as the cloud pictures he and Thunderheart had loved to watch.

The days started to lengthen, and as they lengthened, they seemed emptier. Faolan was diligent in his scent marking so that even if he could not find Thunderheart, perhaps she could find him. But she never came and she did not fade from his memory. Still, Faolan never gave up hope.

In the meantime, he had to go on with the business of living. He had to find meat. He must eat and grow fat as Thunderheart had taught him. Even though he did not sleep through winter, he must be strong and fat to keep the cold away when it came again.

The loneliness of his life grew. Deep within him there was an emptiness that seemed to expand little by little until he felt almost hollow. One day he passed a tree that had been struck by lightning. Its trunk had been scoured out and all that was left was a deep black gash. Its limbs were gray and skeletal, barren of any needles. As he looked at it he realized that he was exactly like that tree. It still stood, but why? It was not living, yet it was not dead. He walked on, the hollowness inside him amplifying with every step. But the hollow steps brought him no closer to Thunderheart.

Faolan continued to hear the howls of the other wolves, but they made no more sense than before. He knew they were wolves, and yet he felt no kinship with them. They might as well have been as different from him as the marmot he had killed a few nights before. Was that what Thunderheart had meant when she said that this place might not be good for his kind?

Faolan preferred to hunt at night, but the nights were becoming shorter and shorter. And when the frost forest seemed to tilt and turn full into the sun, the night simply vanished along with the last remnants of sparkling frost. Thunderheart had told him this happened in the Outermost. There would be no night, no darkness, only sun for the next few cycles of the moon.

On the same day that night disappeared, Faolan began tracking a cougar. Cougars were dangerous. Thunderheart had told him how just before she found Faolan, cougars had killed her cub. They were big — bigger than marmots or wolverines — and fast and cunning. She had told Faolan that he would not be ready to tackle a cougar for a long time. But he felt ready now. And in the back of his mind a strange logic had started to haunt him. *If I can kill the cougar*, he thought, *the cougar who took Thunderheart's cub, maybe she will come back to me.*

He had been tracking the cougar from the time the sun had first risen until it hung low in the sky and seemed to hover endlessly above the horizon like a vigilant golden eye watching the earth. *And so am I,* Faolan thought as he entered the second day of tracking the cougar. The loitering sun inspired him.

It was well into the second day when he began to sense the cougar was tiring, that he was actually closing the distance. But Faolan also became aware of another presence, one that had been following him for a shorter time but was persistent nonetheless. He was immediately wary.

Faolan had developed a quickness of mind that allowed him to concentrate deeply and yet at the same time maintain his alertness. He had caught his first glimpse of his tracker, a tawny smear, behind a thicket of bracken. He was being followed closely now. But he would not be forced off the track of the cougar, nor would he rush the kill.

He spotted the cougar settling down with a hare. The cougar was a bit larger than Faolan, longer and lower to the ground, but it appeared more slender and its chest seemed narrower. Faolan had been careful to maneuver himself into a position downwind of the cougar so his scent would not be carried. He had so skillfully tracked his prey that the big cat was completely unaware of his presence. He was certain, however, that there were two other wolves tracking him. *They want this meat, too. But I'm no raven! I'll not eat second.*

Faolan crept up on the cougar to almost within pouncing distance when a sudden shift in the wind brought his scent to the cat. He saw the flicker of the cougar's nostrils and then the cougar was off. But Faolan was not about to give up. The cougar seemed to be devouring the land in front of him. Faolan kept up. *I will kill you and eat you. I shall grow fat on the meat that devoured Thunderheart's cub. For Thunderheart!* The sound of his feet engulfed him and the thunderous heart of the grizzly became his. There was a thin stand of trees ahead. He had almost reached the cougar when the cat leaped up into the tree.

An image flashed in Faolan's mind. The looming figure of Thunderheart rearing up against a dazzling sun, bright green leaves caught in the last rays as they fluttered down. He leaped now, as he had with Thunderheart. He leaped so high that the cougar made a sound halfway between a snarl and a scream. It was a sound of alarm. But Faolan had clamped on to the cat's paw and dragged him from the limb.

Stunned, for never had a cat been felled in this manner, the cougar could not react quickly enough. Faolan sank his teeth into the vein just beneath the cougar's jaw, the vein that Thunderheart taught him pumped the life-blood and must be cut in order to kill. The cougar twitched once, then again. He was dying.

An instinct rose within Faolan that surprised him. He unclamped his long teeth, and he laid his own head down on the ground so he could look directly into the eyes of the dying cat. They stared at each other for several seconds, and Faolan did not think of Thunderheart. Nor did he think of this animal as a killer of cubs. He thought only of the cougar's grace and speed. And he said, "You are a worthy animal, your life is worthy and shall sustain me."

The cougar peered back into the green eyes of the young wolf. The light in his own amber eyes was growing dim, and yet there was a flicker of recognition. It was as if a coded message passed between them: *I give you permission to take my life. May my meat sustain you.*

CHAPTER ELEVEN

A SAVAGE WORLD

FAOLAN HAD BEGUN TO RIP INTO the flank of the dead cougar when he heard a rustling in the brush. He raised his head, but no longer in expectation of seeing Thunderheart. As soon as he had looked into the eyes of the dying cougar, he had realized that he was mistaken to think that killing the cougar would avenge Thunderheart's cub.

Two wolves stepped out of the brush, the first wolves Faolan had ever seen other than the reflection of his own face in the water. He was stunned. *They are like me, but so different.* He was bigger, much bigger than they were, although they looked older. And they were disreputable, raggedy and unkempt, their coats bearing furless patches that revealed old scars. Both were males, one a dark gray and the other russet. The russet one was missing an eye.

His face was nearly bald on the side with the missing eye, and Faolan knew that the claw marks on it had been made by another wolf. What animal attacked its own kind?

Saliva in long silvery threads dripped from the dark edges of the wolf pair's mouths. They edged closer to where Faolan stood snarling over the carcass. Several things became apparent to Faolan as the trio eyed one another. The two wolves were trying to edge each other out as they moved toward the cougar. Although they had tracked him together, the two were not working as a team. They were not cooperating, maneuvering as he and Thunderheart had in the defile, combining Faolan's swiftness and the grizzly's might to bring down the caribou. They had no strategy.

But Faolan did. The strategy came to him in a quick little burst of insight that flashed in his mind: *They want my meat, but I am not going to let them have it. They will have to fight me, but they don't know how to fight together. Greed means I can distract them.*

Faolan tore out a chunk of cougar meat and tossed it into the air. The two wolves scrambled to pounce on it and fell together in a snarling, tumbling mass. Faolan jumped straight into the air and crashed down on top of them. There was a loud popping sound, then a scream. The dark gray wolf appeared to break in the middle, his lower half skewing to one side and a jagged bone pushing through his pelt. The impact had snapped his spine.

The russet wolf growled and retreated, swinging his head to see with his single eye, which was now darting frantically from the gray wolf to Faolan to the chunk of meat.

Faolan's hackles were raised, his head held high, his ears upright and forward. He took a step toward the russet wolf. The wolf cowered, peeling back his lips in a grimace of fear. But still his one eye kept darting between the chunk of meat and the dead wolf. Faolan was growing impatient and tensed himself to spring, but much to his surprise, the russet wolf ran at the dead wolf and dragged the body into the brush.

Faolan knew he had nothing to fear from the one-eyed wolf, but at the same time he was mystified by his behavior. Why would the wolf drag the body of his friend away? He pricked his ears forward as he heard the rip of flesh. *It can't be!* He walked quietly toward the thicket of brush and peered through the tangled thorny branches.

The russet wolf's head was buried up to its single eye in the ripped belly of the dead wolf. So busy was he consuming the entrails that he wasn't even aware of Faolan's presence for some time. When finally he looked up, his face drenched in the blood and slime of the guts, Faolan saw only greed in that single eye. Laying his ears flat, the russet wolf stepped back, not in shame for his act, but in fear. *He thinks I want his meat!*

Faolan turned away and walked back to the cougar with one thought: *I must eat to get fat. To get stronger.* He would need his strength more than ever. *What kind of savage world have I entered?*

CHAPTER TWELVE

OUTCLANNERS

GUT-HEAVY, THE RUSSET WOLF made his way through a tangled web of scents. He was driven now by a dull sense of fear. He had never seen anything like the silver wolf with the splayed paw. It was not simply that the wolf was large, but he was strong. His chest was broad and the splayed paw, although not especially big, looked powerful. It was lucky that the gray wolf had been on top of him. If not, it would have been his back that snapped. He was frightened now to be alone. He had to find a rout of wolves and travel with them for a bit.

The wolves of the Outermost were unlike any wolves in the entire world. They defied all the common notions of wolf behavior; they were not simply abnormal, but an outrageous insult to the values and traditions that other wolves cherished. Lawless, abiding by none of the elaborate codes of conduct that governed clans and packs, these wolves were known as outclanners.

Notions of honor and loyalty, which were central to the wolves of the Beyond, didn't exist for outclanners. Viciousness and greed were the motivating forces of their lives. Survival was their only instinct. Dulled by generations of savagery, they could never conceive of the intricate strategies that clan wolves had evolved for hunting or living together in the pack spirit of *hwlyn*, nurturing harmony.

The one-eyed wolf known as Morb was no exception. He had swum across the river to rid himself of the gray wolf's blood, for if he attempted to join a rout with the smell of wolf blood all over him, the other wolves might become suspicious. Perhaps if they did smell it, he could claim to have picked up the blood scent in a *craw*, or a fight to the death between two animals. Most times, the combat was between two animals of different species, perhaps a marmot and a wolverine, trapped in a circle formed by the rout, but occasionally the combat was between two wolves. It was peculiar that the only time the wolves of a rout worked cooperatively was not for hunting purposes, but for sadistic amusement. The wolf who won a wolf-to-wolf contest enjoyed a bit of notoriety for a while, but not for long. It was difficult for the outclanners to hold much in their minds for any length of time.

As Morb made his way through the tangle of scents of the dense evergreen forest, he had almost forgotten the scent of Faolan. When the wind shifted suddenly, he did not even realize that the scent he detected was that of the silver wolf he feared. The smell mingled with some others, and Morb thought perhaps there was a rout nearby. Soon he heard some random barks and howls.

It was a *craw*! And a good one at that! A musk ox and an old sick female moose, a cow.

Faolan was a silent moving shadow, his paws soft as moss. He watched transfixed as the wolves pressed in around the musk ox and the moose, one or another darting out to nip at their legs and encourage the big animals to step forward and charge again. One of the musk ox's horns had been broken and was dangling in front of its face, obscuring its vision. This seemed to delight the wolves. The moose was limping and had begun to crouch down. Faolan could see plainly that she was ready to die. But a large, skinny she-wolf with vicious fangs was on her in a minute, goading her to get up. It was a horror that Faolan could have never imagined, even after watching the one-eyed wolf devour his companion.

Faolan stood in the shadows, shivering although it was not cold, his fur rising on his body. Had any of the outclanner wolves glimpsed him, they would have been shocked. Shocked by his size. Shocked by the ferocity in the brilliant green eyes and frightened by a light beneath the ferocity that they could never have named — intelligence.

Faolan considered charging in and busting up the *craw* in hopes that he might afford the moose a peaceful death. But he knew that, in addition to risking his own life, sooner rather than later this rout of vicious wolves would track her down for their own fiendish delight and perhaps kill her in an even more savage manner. And although he felt he could outrun any of these wolves if they did set upon him, it became clear to Faolan that he wanted nothing to do with them at all. He did not want them to know he existed.

So with these thoughts in mind he turned away. As he traveled he remembered those long melodious howls that he had heard outside the winter den of Thunderheart and wondered if perhaps he had heard wrong. The howls of these outclanner wolves were like shards of bone scratching the night. He could not believe that wolves who had howled that beautiful, wild music could ever be the same as these. They must be different, but perhaps they weren't, and yet what did he know about wolves? He had been raised by a grizzly. Then Faolan was struck by an immutable truth, which was that he had more in common with a grizzly bear than any wolf. Surely there would be grizzlies along the river. Or perhaps he would find a lovely summer den above the banks dotted with glacier lilies and irises.

The loneliness that had for so long felt like an empty space within him, that emptiness that had made him feel hollow, grew now until it seemed his own body could not contain it. It seeped out of him and began to create an even bigger hollow, a void, a space that was always at his side. A space where Thunderheart would walk next to him were she still there, a silence that would have been filled had she been snorting and huffing as they made their way to hunt or graze, that unmistakable thump of her immense paws making a track next to his. He wondered how nothingness could feel so heavy. How could hollowness be so crushing? Could the wolves of the

Beyond, the ones whose howling he recalled as distant beautiful songs, ever fill this void? He began to evolve a simple plan. He would find the river, the river that led back into the Beyond. And so Faolan continued on his way, dreaming of summer dens and lazy afternoons fishing for salmon. *Maybe*, he thought, *I could even teach little bear cubs how to fish!*

He had been traveling for a few days when he began to notice that the long light was seeping away little by little and night was returning. It was still high summer — he recognized the thickets of sweet blackberries that grew at this time. But if the endless days were vanishing and night was returning, he knew he must be approaching the border between the Outermost and the Beyond.

He had yet to reach the river when he saw a yawn of darkness ahead. A cave! It was a big cave, perfect for a large animal like Thunderheart. And yet, oddly enough, Faolan could not detect the scent of any creature. The moon was just rising as Faolan stepped inside, and a spike of pale light pricked the darkness of the cave's interior. In the flickering of the moon's silvery light, Faolan caught the image of a four-legged animal that seemed to be running directly out of the stone wall.

Above the animal beat the wings of a bird — a hovering owl. The wall pulsated with life. He could hear the breath of countless creatures. The pounding of hooves, the beating of paws, the stirring of wings. All on the rock of the cave wall.

CHAPTER THIRTEEN

THE BITTERNESS
OF THE OBEA

HOW MANY? HOW MANY HAD IT BEEN? the Obea wondered as she carried this wolf pup in her mouth. This one wouldn't live long. It had been born late in the season, almost midsummer, with just half a hind paw, and it wasn't breathing properly. These late-season pups were rarely normal. The Obea was weary and bitter. She wasn't sure why she felt this way. The winter had been harsh. The earthquake at the cusp of spring had disturbed more than the land; in some strange way the seasons also seemed disrupted. Spring was very late in coming, almost as if it feared to appear amid the aftershocks of the quake. Wildflowers and the moss blossoms that speckled the grasslands seemed to think better of showing themselves until they were sure of a reliable piece of ground that was not going to move. But now the weather was turning, and the Obea's aches and pains were disappearing with the heat of summer. The rancor that she thought had been smoothed away over time, however, began to stir again. Not simply a sharp pebble digging into her paw, it was more animate, coiling inside her like a serpent. She could feel its fangs with every step. *Why me? Why me?*

The whining question over and over again. The Obea never grieved for the pups she carried away, only the ones that she had never given birth to. *Why me? Why me?* The refrain played again through her mind like the moaning of the north wind that swept down from the Outermost.

She began to recall the time when she had first suspected that she might be barren. One mate after the next had left her when she failed to bear pups. After the third mate left, she moved on to a new pack within the same clan. Once she had been considered a beautiful wolf. Her fur was a lustrous tawny gold and she had attracted a fair number of suitors. But as she grew older her pelt had lost its shine. Her teats shriveled until they were the size of hard little pebbles.

She went from pack to pack, until the news had spread and she was forced to seek a new clan. The MacDuncans were good. She had caught the eye of a big black wolf, Donegal MacDuncan. He was an honorable wolf, but it soon enough became apparent that she was not able to bear pups. It was Donegal who asked the clan chieftain, Duncan MacDuncan, if she might become the Obea. It was a kindness really, for at her somewhat advanced age to have to become a lone wolf would have been hard. Still, it was not easy to observe Donegal with a new mate who promptly bore a litter of five healthy pups.

The place of an Obea in the complex social structure of a clan was peculiar. She was rankless, neither high nor low. This meant there was no precise form of conduct for greeting her, for sharing food, or a particular position in the *byrrgis*, the traveling formation the wolves of the Beyond used when they hunted or explored new territory. Nevertheless, she existed on the fringes of the group in much the same way gnaw wolves did, at least until a gnaw wolf was selected for the Watch of the Ring of the Sacred Volcanoes.

The wolves of the pack avoided her. The females were the worst. Some of the females even thought the Obea smelled different, that her scent marks betrayed her barrenness. She knew they talked about her. And when they were heavy with a litter they would often steal furtive glances at her. Some even suspected that she could see through them, right into their wombs, and knew if a pup they were carrying was a *malcadh*. They gossiped that the Obea could actually put a spell on them and cause a *malcadh* to form. The few *malcadhs* who did survive and made their way back to the clan to serve as gnaw wolves suspected that she resented their survival, and avoided her, as if fearful that she might pick them up and carry them away again. And the males, of course, had no interest in her at all. They seemed to look right through her as if she did not exist. She was like air or water, invisible. It had been no life at all for Shibaan.

Well, she must get on with this business. That was what it was for her — a business, a way to earn her keep in the clan. She did her job well, very well indeed. She was clever in finding ingenious *tummfraws*, the sites for abandoning cursed pups. The *tummfraws* that Shibaan found were places frequented by predators or vulnerable to natural disasters, such as river floods or avalanches. If a pup did survive and made it back to a pack in the MacDuncan clan, it proved that he or she was worthy and could become a gnaw wolf and a candidate for the Watch of the Ring of the Sacred Volcanoes. And didn't the wolves of the Beyond owe her, Shibaan? The present chieftain, the Fengo of the Sacred Ring, Hamish was said to be the best Fengo since the original chieftain in the time of the Great King Hoole.

fetch coal from the fires of the Ring of the Sacred Volcanoes. The colliers were expert at diving in the coal beds on the flanks of the volcanoes, and were always hungry. A half-dead pup would be easy prey.

So she dropped the mewling pup. And although in all her years as the Obea she had never turned back to watch a pup, she did now. For the first time, she tried to imagine the moment this creature would die — the sound its tiny bones would make when trampled flat by a long line of migrating behemoths, or its mewl of pain when caught by the grip of an owl's talons. That was a worse thought, a death that would take a long time. First the awful feeling of leaving the ground and then the rip of the owl's sharp talons and beak. The hackles on the Obea's back rose high, and her tail stood straight out from her body. She abruptly swerved off the trail and took the fastest way down a steep slope.

The Obea had not gone far when she felt a slight tremor coming up from the ground. *Not again!* she thought. More aftershocks. But this was worse. Suddenly, the slope opened up before her. There was a great rent in the earth. She stumbled and heard boulders crashing down behind her. And then there was another sound, that of her own bones being crushed.

The Obea was not sure how long she had been unconscious, but by the time she woke, the moon had risen. She looked up into the summer sky that was dusted with stars. She searched out the constellation of the Great Wolf, Lupus, that walked the night toward the Cave of Souls. *I am dying,* she thought, *but will I go to the Cave of Souls? Or* — and she shuddered — *to the dim world?* She had taken those pups all these years to the *tumm-fraws* because it was clan law that she do so. She did not make the laws. She merely had to follow them, and as Duncan MacDuncan always explained, it was for the well-being of the clan. The bloodlines would be ruined if *malcadhs* were allowed to live without a real fight for their lives. The ones who made it, who came back, were exceptional pups and often grew into extraordinary wolves. But wolves were not to grieve over the ones who did not survive. This was the law of the wild. And she had not grieved until now . . . now when she was clearly dying. *Will I be punished? Is there some chieftain higher than Duncan MacDuncan who will turn me away from the Cave of Souls?*

Shibaan was suddenly very frightened. Although the lower half of her body was numb and she felt no real pain, she realized that there was something much worse. It was this new sensation: grief. Grief mixed with fear. Every one of those pups she now began to remember — the first one with the milky eyes, born blind. The one born with only three legs, the earless ones, and tailless ones, and the ones with crooked hips so they could never run. And then there was that one from just the year before with the splayed paw, and the peculiar design on its pad, a swirl of dim lines. For some reason, that pup had unnerved her like none other. She could not get rid of that one fast enough.

There was nothing unnerving or frightening about the little half-paw pup she had abandoned this day. As the numbness crept through her body, she imagined trying to go back and rescue that half-paw pup.

It was as if she were outside the boundaries of her own body. She leaped up the steep slope agilely, hopping over boulders, heading for the moose trail. She was on the trail now, remembering every bend, every pebble. She saw the tiny creature just ahead. Relief swept through her and at the same moment she was conscious of a peculiar sensation, a feeling she had never experienced in the withered teats on her belly. They no longer felt shrunken and hard. *Milk*, she thought. *Milk is coming! I will take this pup and nurse it.* Joy flooded through her. The moose had not come yet. The sky was clear of owls. There was only the spirit trail above.

Duncan MacDuncan, the wise and revered chief of the MacDuncans, stepped out to howl into the night, and told the far-flung packs of his ancient and venerable clan that the Carreg Gaer, the chieftain's pack, was safe after the quake. He had forgotten about the Obea and the mission she had gone on; forgotten, that is, until he tipped his head back to howl. His eyes caught the constellation of the Great Wolf, Lupus, rising in the eastern sky. He watched as a tawny golden mist gathered near the Star Wolf's head. Instantly, he knew it was Shibaan. He had seen her once, long before she joined the MacDuncan clan, when she was young and golden. So he howled his farewell into the vastness of the night. "You have left us, Obea, left us stronger for your sacrifice. Now follow the spirit trail, Shibaan. You have served us well." And then he blinked and this time howled with sheer delight, for a dozen or more little star pups raced from the Cave of Souls to greet her. Another pup followed close behind the Obea, and where his hind paws touched the trail, there was only one little star, as if half its paw were missing.

CHAPTER FOURTEEN

THE CAVE
BEFORE TIME

FAOLAN STEPPED CLOSER TO THE
strange wall with the animal figures. Were these creatures
real or imaginary? *Does the wall breathe or is it merely rock?*
Do I dream or do I wake? These pictures were somewhat
like the star pictures that Thunderheart used to point out
for him with her sharp black claws, but they were so much
more real. He thought he had actually heard the animals
panting as they pounded across the stone. He even went
right up to the wall of rock to sniff it. But it was merely
rock — silent, cold, and unmoving.

Faolan raised his muzzle and began to explore for
scent, any odor that might betray that this was the place
a bear had lived. He would know Thunderheart's smell
anywhere although it differed according to what she was
eating. In spring, there was the wet green fragrance when

she had gorged on plants and bulbs. But there was not a trace of that odor. Nor was there the dry clover smell of summer, or the scent of fish that saturated Thunderheart's fur in late autumn when the salmon ran. It seemed odd to Faolan that so many animals appeared on the walls, looking so real, when the cave was uninhabited.

Uninhabited but not lifeless. Faolan scratched his paw on the hard surface and the glands in his foot released his own scent. *Am I the first animal ever to mark here? How could that be?* He caught sight of another picture and stepped closer to see that it was a spiral — exactly like the one on his splayed paw! He felt his heartbeat quicken and he looked around, folding back his ears. He lowered his tail and began to sink onto his belly in the classic posture of submission. It was the ultimate gesture of respect to a superior power. Although there were no other living animals in this cave, there was a spirit that saturated the very air. It was to that sublime spirit that reverence must be paid.

When Faolan rose up and looked on the cave walls again, he saw there was a picture of the Great Wolf constellation on the ceiling, but with a trail of stars leading up to it. Faolan wondered if there was a place, a sky cave for wolves to travel to after they had lived their lives on earth, like that of Ursulana, the bear heaven where

Thunderheart had said the spirit of her cub had gone. He looked about. *This, too, is a cave. Yet it does not feel like an end, but rather a beginning.*

He felt as if he were on some earthly star trail, a passage to a time before time, when the history of the wolves and owls first became intertwined.

Faolan felt all this, not in the way that he knew how to track an animal or corner a wolverine, or to wait on the upriver side of a rapid during salmon spawning time. No, he knew this in another part of his mind, a part that seemed not exclusively his but part of a consciousness that was larger than the mind of a single wolf. A peculiar kind of knowing that defied boundaries, that was larger than a pack, larger than a clan, beyond even a single species.

This seemingly empty cave bristled with a history vital to Faolan's being. He had been born of a wolf mother and father whom he had never known, raised by a grizzly who had vanished, but if he could learn the mysteries of this cave, he might learn who he really was. And what he was meant to be.

He began to follow the winding path that tunneled deep into the earth. The light grew dimmer and dimmer. But like all wolves he had excellent vision in low light and could see well into the darkest hours of the night.

He pressed closer to the walls, curious to study a silvery streak. He soon realized it was a picture of a luminous flow of wolves, wolves running against a horizon, flowing across a frozen landscape. He felt an overpowering desire to run with these wolves. There was a grace, a majesty as they moved together not as single animals but in this one elemental formation. They were like some earthly, terrestrial constellation. Not cold distant stars but flesh-and-blood wolves so beautifully etched on the rock walls that they seemed to breathe.

Overhead a bird flew. He thought it was an owl. He had not seen many, but when he had, Thunderheart would name them for him. He wished now that he had paid closer attention. For there were several different kinds of owls and Thunderheart had known exactly which kind they were. Some she called Spotted Owls and others Snowy. But the owl that passed over the flow of wolves seemed to be rather the essence of all owls, the spirit of an owl more than a feather and bone and blood owl — just a flash of white cutting the sky.

Faolan lost track of time. He would never know exactly how long he spent in the cave — the Cave Before Time, as he began to think of it. He seemed not to need sleep or food. It was as if he fed on the story that unfolded before him. There were many gaps in the story and the paintings on the other walls did not seem sequential. The first paintings had been of caribou. The flowing line of wolves, which he would eventually learn was called a *byrrgis*, came in the middle, whereas it should have begun the tale. To Faolan, this particular painting was the core of the story. It was the painting that gave him hope, that reminded him of the beautiful howls of the wolves he had heard when he had ventured out from the winter den on those cold nights as Thunderheart slept. It made him realize that not all wolves were like the vicious, stupid ones he had seen in the Outermost.

It was uncanny how the motion of the wolves had been captured by the blurring of their legs. However, it wasn't simply the depiction of the movement that impressed Faolan but rather the sense of joint action, the combined effort of many wolves working together for the sake of one another and the pack. This was completely the opposite of the outclanner wolves he had witnessed in the Outermost. And this was only a fragment of a larger story that he began to piece together in the Cave Before Time.

CHAPTER FIFTEEN

A STORY IN STONE

FAOLAN REMEMBERED THAT THUNDER-
heart had told him of the superior navigation skills of
owls. Whereas most animals only used the North Star,
the polestar, the owls used all the stars. So that was what
he understood first. The wolves were migrating from
the far east to the west and the misty owl was guiding
them. Then other parts of the story began to become
clear.

The wolf in the point position of the *byrrgis* was a
great dire wolf called Fengo, who was the chieftain of
what was then called the Clan of Clans and eventually
came to be known as the MacDuncans. There were other
images throughout the cave of the wolves in this traveling formation. He had seen it perhaps half a dozen times
so far. Usually the formation had been for hunting, but
now it was clear there was another purpose as well. Faolan

could see that the wolves were on the move. He could tell from the paintings that they were leaving a place of ice — Great Ice was how he came to think of it. Over the years, a fierce cold had set in to the country from whence the wolves came and each year stole more and more of the warm times, lengthening the wintertimes, until ice began to creep over the land and cover it for every season of the year. These ancient wolves called this period the Ice March of the Long Cold. The Ice March seemed to follow them everywhere they went in their territory. Fengo, as the leader of the Clan of Clans, decided they must leave. They wandered for many moons, but it was unclear to Faolan when or how they first encountered the spirit of the strange bird.

Faolan suddenly realized that this owl had been called Hoole. He remembered Thunderheart telling him about the extremely intelligent owls who lived on the island in the middle of the Sea of Hoolemere in a tree called the Great Ga'Hoole Tree. He also remembered her saying that *Hoole* was an ancient wolf word for "owl." The name did not seem strange to him but had an oddly familiar ring. As he traced the paintings on the cave walls that twisted and turned down often into deeper recesses and then rose once more, opening into huge galleries with soaring spaces, he followed the spirit of Hoole, who led the wolves to a land he began to recognize as the Beyond. It was a land as wild and desolate as the wolves had ever seen and strange, too, for there was both fire and ice. Hoole had guided them into the eastern region of the Beyond where there was a ring of volcanoes. That was where Fengo and his Clan of Clans first settled.

The cave itself was a maze of tunnels and passageways. It was easy to get lost. And Faolan did for several days. He was never aware of being very hungry. There was water but precious little food. A rat or two, and bats as well. He became quite proficient at plucking off the bats as they slept in their curious upside-down positions. What really fed him were the stories and the paintings themselves, which he found extraordinarily beautiful. He began to develop a discerning eye and a deep appreciation for how the artist expressed the sensations of motion, speed, and weight all on a flat surface.

What still perplexed him, however, was the spiraling design, the same as that on the pad of his splayed paw. He had spotted this design intermittently during his explorations.

Sometimes the passages were blocked. The first time this happened Faolan was quite upset because he was just getting to an interesting part in Fengo's story, after he and his clan had been in the Beyond for several years and he had met an owl who was said to be the first owl to dive for coals, the first collier. The spiral design had also been appearing with greater frequency. Just as he was about to turn back, he felt a slight draft of humid air. Since he was so deep in the cave, it was hard to imagine where it came from. He nosed around a bit and it was not long before he realized that what he thought was a dead end was really a pile of rock chunks that most likely had caved in during the earthquake.

He began digging fiercely. With every clump of rubble that his splayed paw cleared, he thanked Thunderheart for swatting what he had considered his good paw and thus making him use and strengthen the splayed one. He was in a fever now to find out the secret of this spiral design that had marked him.

When Faolan finally cleared away the rubble of the collapse, he passed through into a great bay area that revealed the most magnificent of all the paintings. It was a rounded space that seemed fitting for the subject matter, for he was surrounded by depictions of the five Sacred Volcanoes: Dunmore, Morgan, H'rathghar, Kiel, and Stormfast. Each volcano seemed, upon his first glance, more or less the same. But with closer examination, two had subtle yet distinct differences. Those two, although he could not sense their names at the time, were H'rathghar and Dunmore. Around each one, owls flew, some diving toward rivers of hot embers that spilled down the flanks of the volcano. H'rathghar appeared to be almost translucent, and in its bubbling cauldron Faolan spotted an ember that appeared quite different from those that composed the ember beds of the flanks. This particular ember was orange with a lick of blue tinged with green at its center, the very same green as his own eyes. The ember was cradled in a pocket of bubbling lava. An owl with a white face and tawny feathers appeared to be plunging directly into the cone of the volcano to retrieve the ember. He gasped at the sight. Was this owl intent on killing himself? But then he saw another volcano directly across from this one. It was in a state of violent eruption, and flying out of a curtain of flames was a magnificent owl, this one with many spots, and in his beak he clutched that same enigmatic ember for which the white-faced owl had been diving. Two volcanoes, two owls, both diving through fire for the same ember. What did it signify? Faolan sensed immediately that these two owls were vastly separated in time. But their stories were linked to each other. And to the wolves.

Slowly, Faolan began to circle the space, trying to fit together the pieces of this painted puzzle. At first, he had not noticed the towering mounds of bones. Atop each one a wolf perched. He began to dimly perceive that the wolves were perched on those bone mounds as sentries of some sort. He thought their mission was to protect that ember from the shadow figures that were also flying through the sky. He sensed that these shadow figures were dangerous and treacherous owls. But most frustrating for Faolan, no clue was given as to what the mysterious swirling mark was. It was odd. The marks were scattered throughout but always over the head of an animal. Sometimes a wolf, but sometimes an owl or even a bear, a fox, or a hare.

Faolan exhausted himself trying to decipher the meaning of the mark and he finally fell into a deep sleep in this rounded bay, the vortex of the histories of the wolves and the owls in the Cave Before Time.

CHAPTER SIXTEEN

FIRST MILK

AS FAOLAN SLEPT HE DREAMED, and a scent spiraled through his dreams, entwining itself with the images he had seen in the cave. The scent seemed to flow like the silvery streak of the running wolves. But as it grew stronger he realized this had nothing to do with the runners on the rock wall. He could almost feel squirming soft bodies around him, all of them struggling, fighting toward the warm milky scent. Milk! Milk! Shoving, pushing, vying for a teat in a small dark space that was warm and silent. He could see nothing. He could hear nothing. He could only smell and feel. And when he finally clamped on to that teat he could feel something else. A heartbeat, not the giant pounding one, but a softer, quicker rhythm. He tried to press closer and closer to the light thumping and the milk. A Milk Giver, but so different in this milk dream. And then a cold draft and something pulling on him, the sensation of being wrenched from the teat, pried away from the other struggling, small furry bodies. Coldness, dangling in the air as some creature with no scent at all traveled with him, carrying him away from first warmth, first milk.

Faolan awakened with a yelping bark and stood up, trembling all over. He sniffed the air. There was no scent of milk, but it had been so real! So real!

Although Thunderheart had been very vague about that night she had found him, never mentioning a wolf mother, Faolan knew in one sense that he must have been born of a wolf because he looked so different from the grizzly. But deep within him, Faolan never truly believed it until now. *Is it possible to have two mothers,* he wondered, *the one who birthed you and the one who nurtured you?* The scent of that first one that he had smelled in his dream still lingered in his nostrils and his mind.

He knew that he must leave the cave. The cave was before time. He must enter his time, his territory. He must cross the border into the Beyond and follow the river. He would find his first mother, he would find those little furry bodies that had pressed and wriggled beside him. Why had *he* been taken away and not *them*? He stopped short in his tracks and stared down at the splayed paw. He picked it up, then twisted down on his shoulder so he could fix his eyes on the swirled print of the pad. This was why!

But oddly enough, a great peace stole over Faolan. He did not know the word *malcadh*, "cursed one." But it was not cursed that he felt, nor was it blessed. Instead, it seemed as if he had a glimmering that he was part of something larger, a larger pattern, a larger plan, an endlessly spiraling harmony. Darkness was falling around him, and Faolan held his paw up to the new moon, which was rising. A low cloud swept out on either side of the silver blade like a great luminous bird hovering on the horizon.

The stars began their stately climb in the growing blackness of the night. He watched silently and began to realize that the movement of the stars was like the flow of running wolves. They did not move separately; their transit was in concert. They were part of something larger, and it seemed as if the sky, too, turned around the earth, which might be just another star that also turned, a very small piece in a single sliding whole. *Around and around, just as these marks on my paw. I belong to the endless cycle.*

CHAPTER SEVENTEEN

THE *BYRRGIS* OF ONE

FAOLAN HAD BEEN TRAVELING for several days. The moon that had been a thin blade when he had come out of the cave had swollen to an immense silvery sphere. He had seen no other wolves, heard no howls. During the heat of the day he often lay down on a cool rock by the river and then in the late afternoon he would begin to swim in search of fish. But he was beginning to crave real meat. The woods along the river had grown sparser and one day he followed a trail up from the riverbank to a broad plain. It was twilight and an indigo glow began to fill the evening. Faolan rammed his ears forward. There was an odd clicking noise that he picked up on the breeze. He had heard it before with Thunderheart; he knew the sound. Caribou! The muscles in their legs snapped as they trotted along. They were moving to their calving grounds.

The juices in his stomach seemed to surge. He could taste blood already, but there was no Thunderheart to help, no defile in which to trap a caribou. The strategy that had worked so well in the past was useless here. But he had killed a cougar. It was just a single cougar and this was an entire herd. He would have to single out the weak one and then pursue it. His mind went back to the cave — the magnificent stream of wolves floating over the landscape, working together with great purpose. A river of scents now poured toward him, carried on the wind. He could do this even if he was alone.

Faolan began traveling toward the scent, careful to keep downwind. There was a sea of tremulous vibrations that began to rise from the ground and grow stronger, and soon he spotted the herd breaking out from behind a bluff. They were in the open now and moving into the central part of the plain that dipped into a shallow valley. It was not a defile but still it offered advantages. He could stay slightly above the herd and downwind. It would give him a view from which he could survey the herd and pick out a weak member. He felt sleeker and faster than he had a few moons earlier, for his winter underfur had begun to shed. Swiftly, he climbed a rocky ridge and, moving along it, studied the flow of caribou. Two ravens circled above him. He sensed they were waiting for him to attack the herd. He was annoyed. He didn't want the circling ravens to give away his location. But the herd moved along mindlessly, relentlessly, at a steady pace as inexorable as the course of a river.

Faolan soon caught sight of an elderly cow at the edge of the herd. He could tell that she was having trouble keeping pace. This was his target. Stealthily, he made his way down the slope. There was a sudden but slight wind shift. The clicking of the caribous' tendons quickened as they picked up their pace. *They smell me*, Faolan thought. He watched the cow attempt to make her way to the center of the herd, but she was shoved once again to the edges. He was a good distance behind the herd, which had more than doubled its speed. The cow was running faster, too. She was perhaps not as infirm or old as Faolan thought. But he restrained himself from accelerating. *Not yet*, he thought. *I must keep a steady pace. Act as if I am not one alone, but one of many.*

He loped along, keeping his eyes on the cow. Instinctively, he knew that in the *byrrgis* the females were the fastest and therefore ran in the front of the formation. But he would have to cover all positions and therefore he must carefully gauge not only the caribou's speed, but also his own energy.

The herd had been heading up a slight incline and it

was here that the cow decided to split from them as she knew she could not keep up on a slope. She turned and picked up speed as she headed in another direction. Faolan veered to follow her. The flat of the terrain renewed the cow's energy. She was pressing on at an admirable clip, but Faolan could hear the roughness of her breathing. She could not keep this up forever.

Or could she? he thought sometime later. He had been tracking her over a great distance for a long time. Stars had risen and slid down the other side of the black dome of the night. The moon was now on the distant horizon. And still her pace was steady. *But I am not alone,* he thought, and remembered again the flowing line of wolves. Each wolf had a part to play in the formation, whether they were migrating or hunting. When he had stood close to the rock wall and gazed for hours, there were moments when he had felt as if he was truly part of that flow of wolves. Now he could almost feel the presence of scores of fleet animals pressing in around him, and then other times the wolves would stretch out in a long swift stream as they silently signaled one another in this phantom *byrrgis* of many, of which Faolan was just one. *One in all. All in one!*

He must let the caribou cow think that he had given

up. He scanned the landscape. There was a dip ahead and then beyond it a hill, not big but big enough. If he could fool her, then he could come from around the other side and force her to head for the incline.

He gave a short, breathy series of huffs followed by a howl and turned tail. There was a sudden pocket of quiet in the night. The sound of the clicking tendons ceased. Faolan turned around slowly, almost elaborately. He felt the cow watching him. He disappeared into the dip and then circled around behind a low bluff. The cow had slowed to a walk. There was no defile to trap her, but if he could force her toward the slope . . .

He acted fast, so she had no time to recover. He bolted out from behind the bluff he had just circled and chased her up the incline in a tremendous burst of speed. She was only halfway up when he gave a great leap, slamming his front paws onto her hips to bring her down. He scrambled on top of her and secured a jaw hold on her neck. Then, peeling back his dark lips, he sank his teeth into the neck, crushing her windpipe. He wanted her to die fast, but not too fast. Once again, as with the cougar, he had an urge to acknowledge her strength, her endurance. She needed to know that he respected her, that he felt her worthy. The instinct for *lochinvyrr* was a compulsion as old as wolves. He was desperate to look into this dying caribou's eyes. He wanted her to know that he valued her life, her gift to him. If this could happen the meat would be *morrin*, sanctified. It would be with good purpose that the caribou had died. Faolan knew none of this; it was only ancient instinct that guided him as the cow lay dying.

There was a flicker of light in the old cow's eyes as she looked directly into Faolan's. He heard the crackle of the last breath in her broken windpipe. *I have lived a long life, a good life. I have calved and run with the herd. I am ready to go, to let go. My time is over.* It was as if the two animals nodded to each other, and then the caribou died.

CHAPTER EIGHTEEN

A First Drumlyn

THE RAVENS BEGAN TO CIRCLE overhead before the caribou had taken her last breath. It irritated Faolan. It was not selfishness or hunger that made him growl as two pairs settled on a rock a short distance from the carcass. It was not even the fact that he had been the one to bring down the caribou and they wanted to feast on his hard work. It was rather the notion of these rackety birds with their harsh *kras* pecking at the meat of this noble animal. It disturbed him deeply. There was still meat left and Faolan had more than satiated his hunger, but the idea of the ravens sickened him. He decided to take the carcass to a place where it would be safe from scavengers.

He began dragging the body by its antlers across the flat, treeless plain. The ravens followed and when he paused or rested they would light down. But Faolan was a relentless sentry. He bared his teeth, revealing the long fangs that the birds had originally counted on for ripping open the tough hide of the caribou. The ravens found his behavior bewildering. Normally, after wolves had their fill they left the rest for the birds. It was why ravens were often known as wolf birds, for they followed the packs.

As Faolan hauled the body across the plain, an idea came to him. He recalled the times when he and Thunderheart looked out onto the summer nights, and the grizzly told him the stories of the star pictures. In particular, he remembered the night she had told him of Ursulana, the bear heaven to which the constellation of the Great Bear pointed and where she was sure that her cub's spirit had gone. In the Cave Before Time, he had begun to think that there might be a refuge for the spirit of wolves as well. It now occurred to Faolan that perhaps there was a starry refuge for the spirits of caribou. The thought quickened his pace.

A bold raven swooped down toward the caribou. He was still quite high, however. Faolan was incensed and leaped up and snatched the bird right out of the air. The five other ravens were so stunned that they stalled in their flight and began to plummet toward the ground. Never had they seen a four-leg soar so high. Faolan had killed his raven instantly. The others recovered from their near fatal plunges and flew off. That was the last Faolan saw of them.

It had been Faolan's intention to drag the body of the caribou to the high banks of the river, to a spot far from the fishing grounds frequented by animals during the salmon spawning season, and far from the shallow crossing points used by migrating herds. He knew that such places were favored by predatory animals for bringing down moose, caribou, deer, and musk oxen. He was determined that no creature should touch these bones while there was still meat on them. He would finish eating what he could, and then he would hide the bones.

At last Faolan found a good spot high above a deep place in the river. The calm surface water concealed treacherous currents, making it a precarious place for migratory animals to cross. Furthermore, he had not picked up the slightest trace of scent. Fox families would have been frightened that their kits might fall off the edge. Wolverines preferred dens at the bottom of steep rock slides or at the very top of talus slopes. They were skillful at finding sheltered spaces between the rocks. Martens and weasels liked the deep forest. This place was perfect.

He was hungry again from the labor of dragging the caribou. Soon, he had stripped a few bones clean. He had even scraped the hide clean and then curled up on it to rest. There was a moment just before twilight when the moon rose in the east like a ghost of itself just as the sun set in the west. Then the night unfolded, first tingeing the air violet. The violet deepened to purple and then the purple to black as the constellations climbed in the sky. Faolan tipped his head up and began to howl, calling to the stars.

Show me the shelter
in the sky
for the noble caribou.
Show me the starry path she must travel.
Her way is the way of honor —
she is caribou.
I am wolf.
I live because she died.
She is goodness,
I am humble beneath this silver night.

I beg — show me the way,
and I shall put her bones to rest.

Faolan howled until late in the night. There was not a breath of wind and when he first spotted the antlers of the caribou constellation, it was not in the sky but in the reflection of the moon-polished river. The surface quivered slightly, like the spreading limbs of silver trees in a breeze. Faolan stepped closer to the edge and looked straight down. His pulse raced with excitement as the constellation rose in the night and he traced the familiar profile of the caribou — starting with its antlers, then its head, dwarfed by the lofty height of those branching horns. He followed the slight scoop of the neck flowing back to the meaty hump that rose above the shoulders. It took six stars to make those large concave hooves. Faolan began to howl again.

Follow! Follow!
Follow the star caribou.
Follow her to the spirit shelter.
Find your mother who died in the winter,
your father felled by the bear.
Gather with the spirit herd —

they wait for you
in the star-splashed night.

And when he finished howling, he looked down on the stripped bones glistening in the moonlight. An urge thrust up from deep inside him. It was a new kind of hunger, not for food, not for blood, but simply to gnaw, to create something beautiful on these gleaming bones like the images inscribed on the rock walls in the Cave Before Time. This overpowering urge was one that all gnaw wolves, those pups who although abandoned had survived, seemed to possess — a fierce compulsion to gnaw on stripped bones. Not all gnaw wolves, however, perceived so clearly the possibility of the beauty they could create, or kept it so firmly in their mind's eye as Faolan seemed to. He could envision precisely what he had to do to make these etch marks into a powerful design.

The instinct was not only to gnaw but to inscribe on the bones designs that were sometimes stories and sometimes simply art with no beginning, middle, or end. If a gnaw wolf was selected for the Watch at the Ring of the Sacred Volcanoes, the bones they gnawed were piled on top of others from centuries before and the mounds that formed were called *drumlyns*. The wolves of the

Watch perched on these *drumlyns* in their vigils at the Ring of the Sacred Volcanoes. Faolan had seen such mounds in the painting in the cave. Whether he remembered them now did not matter. He had never gnawed a bone like this before but he instinctively knew what to do. For he was filled with this urge to gnaw a design, a message for the star caribou. And with this urge came a yearning to be with his own, to find wolves.

By the time the dawn broke, Faolan had started his first *drumlyn*, though he did not know the word. He perched atop it and began to howl at the dawn. The rising sun broke on the horizon, fracturing the surface of the river into shards of light — rose, burnt orange, blood red. The river glittered fiercely as Faolan sang his wild song — a song of farewell.

PART THREE

THE BEYOND

CHAPTER NINETEEN

THE SKULL IN
THE WOODS

FAOLAN HAD HOWLED HIS FAREWELL
to the spirit of the caribou. He was certain the spirit had
found its way to the shelter just beyond the starry tips of
the constellation's antlers. He did not leave the *drumlyn*
immediately but lingered for several days, gnawing new
designs in the empty spaces on a thigh bone or a shoulder
or rib. He had learned how to use his shearing teeth deli-
cately, so that only the finest lines were inscribed. Had he
heard the howling of other wolves he would have moved
on to join them. But he heard none. However, he felt certain that he must have crossed over the border of the
Outermost into the Beyond, and the wolves here would
be like the ones he had heard when he was at the winter
den with Thunderheart. But he never heard any. He had
meticulously scent marked the surrounding territory of

the *drumlyn* so no animals would trespass. But certainly if there had been wolves in the vicinity he would have heard them.

In addition to the absence of wolves, there were very few other animals. This spot where he had erected the *drumlyn* and where he had passed much of the summer seemed quite isolated. When he went to hunt he had to travel a fair distance if he wanted large animals like caribou. And he had gone hunting, adding the bones of his prey to the original ones of the cow. So now the *drumlyn* rose to a fairly respectable height.

It was hard to leave this peaceful place that had become the earthly point of departure for the caribou, but as the summer waned and the earth tilted farther away from the sun, the caribou constellation slid farther down in the western sky until finally one night, only the tips of the antlers rose above the horizon. Faolan knew that by the next evening the constellation would disappear completely. It was time to go. The days were shortening. Autumn was coming. He needed to find a winter den.

No, he thought. *I need to find a pack of wolves.* He recalled vividly the paintings on the walls of the Cave Before Time. He so wanted to be part of something larger and something better than those routs of outclanner wolves.

In the Cave Before Time, he had seen two constellations of wolves. One was the starry one on the rock ceiling. The other "constellation" was not stars but the hunting and traveling formation of wolves running together. In that formation he had sensed a common feeling, a spirit of fellowship. It made him feel all the more lonely. He had wanted to run with those wolves, to be part of that "constellation," ever since he had first seen the picture. But what if he was rejected?

At the same time he wanted to find Thunderheart. Could he live in both worlds — that of his beloved grizzly and that of the wolves? he wondered. The thought of Thunderheart dying was unimaginable to him. He could not even permit himself to think such a thing. For this reason, when he had scanned the skies for the constellation of the caribou each summer night he would not let his eyes rest on the Great Bear. He knew his instincts were selfish. But as much as he missed Thunderheart's presence beside him in a den or out hunting or fishing, it was quite another thing to imagine her not sharing this earth with him. The distance between here and Ursulana was simply too great. Thunderheart had called Ursulana "heaven," but for Faolan, it felt like the dim world.

Faolan knew that he must leave this place now, before

the horizon swallowed the last star tips of the caribou antlers. So he began walking away in the direction from which the river flowed. He looked back one last time at the mound of bones burnished by the moon's light.

He traveled around a big bend in the river. The bend was one he did not remember at all, but he soon found a good place to cross. Upon climbing up the steep bank on the other side, he smelled a familiar scent in the breath of the river. He began to run. He recognized this odor and saw the water boiling with the silvery bodies of fish leaping in the morning sun. It was the salmon spawning run and just ahead were the same rapids where he and Thunderheart had stood catching fish after fish. He cringed now when he saw another grizzly in the spot, standing with three cubs. The cubs did not notice him, but the mother did and looked at him warily. Faolan's heart seemed to skip a beat. He felt a strange mixture of disappointment and relief. Disappointment that it was not his beloved Thunderheart but also relief, for he could not have borne the thought of Thunderheart with new young ones. He wanted no other cubs sleeping close to that great booming heart.

The grizzly gave a soft snarl of warning. Faolan lowered his tail and dipped his head to signal: *Don't worry. I will not harm your cubs.* The bear understood perfectly.

She had blinked because for just a moment the small movement of the head was so essentially bear that it was hard to believe that the wolf was not one despite his appearance.

It had been a long time since Faolan had tasted salmon, but desolation chased away his hunger. He yearned for Thunderheart more than ever but was glad to know that now he was truly back in the Beyond. The rapids of the salmon run confirmed this. *This is where I belong*, he thought. *I am a wolf of the Beyond*. But there was little conviction in his heart that accompanied this thought.

He moved on through another day and two more nights. He began intermittently to hear the distant howl of wolves, as welcome as they were intimidating. He understood them, but they served to remind him of how different he was. When the grizzly at the salmon rapids had blinked at him, he had seen the confusion in her eyes. *What are you?* she seemed to say.

Faolan had to ask himself the same question. He was a wolf of sorts, but would other wolves accept him? The farther he traveled, the more uncertain he became.

He saw signs of the devastation that the earthquake had wrought. Indeed the course of the river seemed to have been altered, as many new creeks ran from it where he had never remembered them before.

He sensed that the summer den that he and Thunderheart had shared had been flooded by one of these countless new creeks, for there was no sign of it. The thicket of alders now stood in water halfway up the tree trunks. There was no sign of the glacier lilies or the blue drifts of irises. And yet there was a familiarity about the woods that made him ache with those first memories of Thunderheart.

The woods became denser but were riddled with small streams and creeks that had gurgled up since the earthquake. Faolan was about to step into the shallows of a stream when the sunlight glinting off a polished black stone caught his attention. He lowered his head to poke it with his muzzle, for he thought it looked pretty. He quickly noticed that there was a spiraling pattern almost exactly like the one on the pad of his forepaw. He stopped and gripped it in his teeth to pick it up, but carefully, so as not to mark it. He dropped it on the bank and stared at it for a long time. There was an odd comfort in discovering this design, such a part of him, inscribed on stone.

He gently placed the stone back into the stream, then turned and walked on.

The sun began to sink, a cold blue light stealing through the forest and strips of milky mist swirling around the dark pines. There was an eerie paleness to the woods, as if Faolan had entered a region that was neither earth nor sky. He could feel the ground underfoot and yet wraithlike swags of fog wrapped the dark tree trunks so that they seemed to float. He proceeded warily, his ears forward, his tail slightly raised, and his hackles straight up and bristling.

There was something white ahead, whiter than the swaths of fog. Blazing white. At first he saw only fragments of this whiteness. As shapeless as the fog that swirled around him. But as he drew closer, the whole of it revealed itself, and he realized what it was — the skull of a majestic grizzly. He staggered briefly and then rushed toward it — the skull of his beloved Thunderheart rose in the blue milky light of the forest with a majesty that made Faolan drop to his knees.

For long minutes he stared into the empty sockets, his own eyes thick with tears. He did not see death, only grandeur in that skull of the great grizzly, that skull that had breathed life into him. He saw only beauty in those bones. Then he tipped his head up to the sky, now indigo and splattered with stars, and searched for the Great Bear.

When he found the constellation, he threw back his head and began to howl. He howled her to Ursulana. All night he howled and watched the stars and the sliding spectacle of the blue night.

In the Cave Before Time, Faolan had seen that time spiraled back into an unimaginable mist with no beginning and no perceivable end. Now, scanning the starry path to Ursulana, he began to realize that the earth on which he was standing was simply another star in what might be an infinity as vast as time. *In all that time, in all the stars, Thunderheart and I came together for one moment in this never-ending cycle. There are other stars, other universes, and so much time, and yet . . .*

> *Cycling, cycling forever*
> *bear, wolf, caribou.*
> *When had it all started, where will it end?*
> *We are all part of one,*
> *from such simple beginnings*
> *and yet all so different.*
> *Yet one.*
> *One and again,*
> *Thunderheart eternal*
> *now and forever!*

CHAPTER TWENTY

AN OWL LISTENS

GWYNNETH, A MASKED OWL, TURNED the tongs in the fire. This was her third attempt to make a metal replica of a willow leaf. There was not a willow leaf, nor a willow tree, anywhere in the Beyond. And it was not the kind of item for which there was much of a demand. Rogue smiths mostly set their hammer and tongs to making practical articles — pots, kettles, battle claws, and various weapons. But there had been a decline in the need for weapons since the end of the War of the Ember. Her late father, Gwyndor, who had died as a result of wounds in that war, had been a highly regarded smith specializing in double-action battle claws. Gwynneth had a more artistic turn of mind and had learned much of her craft from her auntie. Not her real auntie, but a Snowy Owl who refused to use her talents for military purposes, and devoted herself almost entirely to artistic endeavors. It would have perhaps served the Snowy well to have made a few claws to keep around her forge, for she had been murdered by Nyra, the vicious leader of an empire of hellish owls known as the Pure Ones.

Gwynneth would have taken over her auntie's old forge in the ruins of a walled garden, but it felt odd to her after the Snowy had been killed. Almost as if the Snowy was looking over Gwynneth's shoulders every time she took up the tongs.

Rogue smiths were known for their solitary ways. They liked living apart. On occasion they came to the Ring of the Sacred Volcanoes to barter for coals from the volcanoes. And if a forest fire broke out, Rogue smiths might set up temporary forges on its fringes. But for the most part, they sought out desolate places. It was unusual for Rogue smiths to have mates, or children for that matter. Gwynneth never knew her mother, but her father had had a close relationship with the Snowy and would leave his daughter with her for great stretches of time.

And Gwynneth had grown to love them both, although each was very different. When her father worried about her "going all artsy on him," he would take her to the Beyond. Over the years, Gwyndor had developed a very close relationship with wolves. He had learned their ways and, most important, his ear had grown finely attuned to their howling. He had come to realize that his daughter, Gwynneth, had an even sharper ear for wolf songs and had decided to teach her all he knew. She was an apt pupil. She knew the pitch of every *skreeleen*, the lead howler. But the *skreeleen* varied depending on the situation. Whereas Gwyndor could only pick out the gist of the message, Gwynneth could decipher much more. She was close to fluent in the songs of the wolves.

Gwynneth was in the midst of her third attempt at the willow leaf when she heard the eerily beautiful howling. She withdrew the tongs immediately and set them on the stone rest.

The song went straight to her gizzard. It was a song of grief, yet also one of acceptance, being sung by no *skreeleen* she had ever heard.

Gwynneth damped the fire in her forge and put her tools away. She fought an urge just to toss the tools into a heap, for she was nearly desperate to find the source of this song. But such behavior was unthinkable. Her father and auntie had taught her that a smith is only as good as her tools. Rusty tools led to rusty skills and rusty skills made for *skart*, which was an owl obscenity that covered many things, including inferior products made by poor smiths.

But it did not take Gwynneth long to tidy up, and perched now on the stone rest where her tongs had been, she spread her wings to take advantage of the warm drafts coming up from the smoldering coals in the forge. On these crisp autumn nights, having a boost for takeoff from a thermal draft was nothing to sniff at.

Seconds later, she was skimming the treetops. Taking a bearing on the second star in the Golden Talons, she veered and flew a course two points to the south. The howls rose through the night, a filigree of sound inscribing the wind. Gwynneth had flown a league or more when she spotted the young wolf in a funnel of moonlight. She alighted deep in the branches of a tree to listen.

Though Gwynneth understood the phrases of the song, something confused her. From behind a screen of pine needles, she could see that the wolf, a male, had stationed himself by a large skull of a grizzly. It was to this grizzly that the wolf was singing with such passion. But what was the meaning of that phrase that he howled? "We are all part of one . . ."?

Gwynneth listened carefully as the wolf launched into a second *gwalyd*:

Milk Givers, Milk Givers,
do you both walk the sky,
climb the ladders to starry caves
and wait for me to die?
When my time comes to leave
where shall my spirit walk?
For am I wolf or bear?
I know not where to start.

When the wolf's howling ended, Gwynneth saw him slide the side of his face into a patch of earth near the grizzly's skull and begin to rub his head and his neck vigorously. Gwynneth recognized it as a scent roll, in which the wolves announced a territorial claim. But this wolf did not plan on hunting. Far from it, especially if one considered the keening lament at the heart of his song. By this time, the wolf was dashing about the skeletal remains and rolling wherever he could, as close as he could to the bones. She began to suspect that the wolf had detected perhaps a second aroma. And then it came to her in a sudden flash — two Milk Givers. Two mothers.

CHAPTER TWENTY-ONE

A FIRESIDE CONVERSATION

"WE HAVE MUCH IN COMMON," Gwynneth said, swooping down from the tall pine and alighting a respectful distance from the skull. Faolan looked up. He held a bone from what had been the paw of Thunderheart in his teeth and stared at the Masked Owl.

"Put the bone down, dear, and follow me." Almost as soon as Gwynneth said the words she realized her error. Faolan shook his head vigorously.

"No, of course not. Your milk mother's bone. Bring it with you, but follow me." She spread her wings and lofted herself into the air.

Faolan looked up. When the owl had first appeared, he had been confused by his overwhelming grief. But slowly he realized that an owl, possibly an owl from the Great Ga'Hoole Tree, had actually spoken to him. He rose on wobbly legs and began to follow her flight.

Faolan was amazed at how quiet she was even as she flapped her immense wings in takeoff. So much quieter than the ravens. This was perhaps what drew him to her. Her quietness. It soothed him in his grieving. He wanted to be near her. It was Thunderheart who had first told him of the intelligent owls of Ga'Hoole.

Tipping his head up, he watched the dark silhouette of the Masked Owl's wings printed against the full moon. He began to slip through the blue shadows of the trees and every few paces he would lift his head up to follow the owl's flight against the sweep of the stars. It was not long before he picked up the scent of smoke from her smoldering forge.

When he first saw the fire in the Masked Owl's forge he backed away. He had only seen fire once, from a distance, when he was first learning to fish with Thunderheart. It had been an immense forest fire. The smoke had turned the day to night, and the flames, like red claws, shot up as if to tear the sun from the sky. This fire was hissing and spitting sparks. There were crackling sounds as well that reminded him of the small bones of prey he had caught in his jaws. The crackling noise was punctuated by an occasional loud snap and a hiss.

"Come, come," the Masked Owl said. "It's safe. The fire will not leap from my forge. Don't worry." She took out her tongs. With a slightly alarming twist of her head, she indicated to Faolan that he should make himself comfortable near the fire with his bone.

Suddenly, there were several new sounds, sounds he had never heard before. The clank of the iron tongs, the crackling of the fire, the huff of the wind-catcher claws that the Masked Owl squeezed and pointed at the embers in the fire to bring the flames to life.

"What are those claws?" asked Faolan, his ears tilted toward her.

Gwynneth turned around and churred softly to herself. "These? These are bellows. I'm a Rogue smith. A blacksmith. I craft things out of iron and metals."

"What kinds of things?" Faolan asked.

"I'll show you. But first we should introduce ourselves." Gwynneth wanted to hear this wolf speak some more. His howling had been unique, and so was his speaking voice. There was a curious roughness to it, not unlike the soft trilling burr of the clan wolves. Yet there was something different. No one, however, would ever mistake him for an outclanner. His ways were somewhat formal. He had a grace, a dignity that usually came with being raised in a pack where one was taught to respect rank, order, and, most important, one's elders.

Gwynneth had noticed the malformed front paw immediately and surmised that he had been cast out from the pack yet had survived. So where had he acquired these qualities, these manners that were so much a part of the wolf world? The two Milk Givers? A reference, even an indirect one, to these Milk Givers would perhaps open the conversation. That could be her "first strike," as they said in the parlance of Rogue smiths — the first strike was the first blow of the hammer when the metal had been heated sufficiently.

"My name is Gwynneth. I was named for my mother because she died before I hatched. Another owl had to sit the egg. She also helped raise me. She sometimes called me Gwynnie. And what is your name?"

The wolf was suddenly alert. He dropped the bone for the first time and peered hard at the owl.

"Faolan. She called me Faolan." Gwynneth did not have to ask who "she" was. It was the grizzly bear. He moved a bit closer, with his paws still on the bone. "Your mother died? Another took care of you?"

"Helped care for me and taught me the craft of smithing," Gwynneth replied.

"So you had a father and a second mother?" Faolan asked.

"Yes, I said we had a lot in common."

Faolan crept even closer now to the fire with his bone. He had never felt this kind of warmth before. The fire itself was a landscape. The flames danced in a wind of their own. Like trees, they grew out of the bed of glowing coals that were their earth. The snaps and crackles of the fire often were accompanied by explosions of starry sparkles. It was not just a landscape, but a world — an entire universe.

As he stared into the fire, Faolan began to speak slowly in his rough, lilting voice. It sounded to Gwynneth as if he had not conversed in a long time. His voice scraped, creaked a bit like the rusty hinges the Masked Owl sometimes pried from the doors of the Others' ruins to melt down for her fires.

"I don't know who my father was. I think I have a milk memory of my mother. Just her scent, that is all. But there is more than a milk memory of Thunderheart."

"Thunderheart?"

"Yes, she raised me." Faolan paused a moment and then began to speak again, but now it was as if the hinge broke in two. His voice cracked. "She left . . . I don't know why."

"Thunderheart was a bear, wasn't she? A grizzly."

Faolan dragged his eyes from the fire and nodded. Something touched him deeply when Gwynneth spoke the grizzly's name out loud. He had never heard it spoken aloud by any creature other than himself. His paws rested on the bone and then he laid his head atop his paws and gazed at Gwynneth. "She left. That was her skull and now I only have this . . . this bone." He licked the bone. "She would hold me in her arms while I nursed, hold me close with her huge paws and I could hear her booming heart."

"And so you called her Thunderheart," Gwynneth said quietly.

"Yes." He raised his head now. "Did your father leave you? Did your second mother as well?"

"My father died in war. My second mother was murdered."

"What is murdered?"

"She was killed for no reason — not prey for food or for a cause."

"But she didn't leave you. Not your second mother or your father. Neither one of them left you."

"And I don't think either your first mother or Thunderheart left you."

"But my first mother did leave me," Faolan said

stubbornly. "And I was found by Thunderheart. If it hadn't been for Thunderheart —"

Gwynneth interrupted. "You were taken from your first mother."

"Taken!" Faolan, suddenly alert, raised his head. Every hair in his ruff stood out.

"Faolan, I learned the craft of smithing from my second mother. But I learned the ways of wolves, the wolves of the Beyond, from my father, Gwyndor."

"Tell me then. Tell me about the wolves and why I was taken," Faolan pleaded. The burr in his voice thickened. His gleaming green eyes were fixed on the bone of Thunderheart.

And so Gwynneth told him about the Obea and how when a *malcadh* was born it was required by ancient wolf laws to take the pup and leave it to die. That the mother and the father were driven from the pack.

The sky grew darker, and in the folds of the night by the Rogue smith's fire, Faolan listened while Gwynneth explained the ways of the wolves. As he listened, he began to gnaw on the bone of Thunderheart lightly, the delicate etching noises threading through Gwynneth's words.

"But if that wolf pup lives it may rejoin the pack as a gnaw wolf."

"A gnaw wolf? What's that?"

Gwynneth waited a moment before answering and cocked her head to look at the lines Faolan had etched on the bone. "It is what *you* have become, but your designs are beyond your years, almost better than any I have ever seen, even at the *drumlyn* of Hamish, the Fengo of the Watch."

When she said those last words there was a familiar resonance to them, as if Faolan had heard them somewhere before. Not heard them! Seen them! He recalled the paintings on the cave walls where the five volcanoes were depicted — the towering mounds, the *drumlyn* with a wolf perched atop each one. It was as if he had not just seen those paintings, but lived them in some dim, misty time.

"So if I return I am to become a gnaw wolf?"

Gwynneth tipped her head straight up, then straight down. Faolan had never seen a bird or any animal able to move its head in the peculiar way an owl did.

"Yes," she replied. "And it's hard."

"But you say I am good at it."

"That will make it harder for you."

"I don't understand."

"They treat gnaw wolves especially roughly when they

first return. Other young wolves will be jealous. You need to prove yourself."

"Isn't being abandoned, carried away, and expected to die, rough enough? Haven't I proven enough already?" He paused and muttered something almost unintelligible in a deep reverberating tone that sounded quite bearish. Indeed it was the old bear oath that Thunderheart often growled when she was irritated. Urskadamus, curse of a rabid bear.

He sighed deeply. "So my first mother, my first Milk Giver did not leave me. I was taken. But what about my second, Thunderheart?"

Gwynneth blinked her dark eyes. "You don't mean to say that you think that Thunderheart abandoned you?"

"It's not like with wolves and Obeas. No one takes things from a grizzly bear," Faolan replied evenly.

Gwynneth was caught up short by the young wolf's response. Of course it was absolutely true. No creature in his or her right mind would try to take anything from a grizzly. "She did not leave you, Faolan. You must stop that kind of thinking right now."

"Then why did she go away?" Faolan shoved his ear forward, and his hackles rose up. He was quivering with a new terror, a possibility he had never really thought of, or faced. The emptiness that had become an omnipresent space beside him seemed now to engulf him. It almost radiated with not just his loneliness, but his fear that he was completely and forever unlovable.

This terror came with its own shadow and the bright reflections of the flames from Gwynneth's fire, which had moments before filigreed the darkness with bright orange light raked with sparks, seemed to be quenched. The very air turned darker.

"Maybe she went to find you. To search for you. Maybe she thought you were lost." He cringed and pulled his lips back so they cleared his teeth. Fear and shame coursed through him. It all made a terrible kind of sense now. He had found the winter den boring. He could not believe how much Thunderheart slept. The thickness of her sleep lay like a heavy pelt on the air of the den. Sometimes he had to get out — to run, hunt. He loved leaping through the big soft drifts of snow. And he remembered how slowly her heart beat. Not the familiar booming rhythm, but softer, sluggish. He could get up and turn around two times then snuggle back down against her between the beats of that slow heart. And every once in a while she would wake up, groggy and slightly confused. If he had been out on a run when she woke, she might have

165

panicked and gone out to find him. The shadow of the void, that omnipresent space retreated a bit. The terror grew slightly dimmer, the flames once more threaded the black with glints and winks of light.

"You are right. She left to search for me because sometimes I would get bored in the winter den. She must have forgotten that she told me it was all right to go out and hunt sometimes."

"The cold sleep is the way of bears."

"Yes, and she knew I wasn't a bear." Faolan paused. "But . . ." He could not finish the thought.

"But what, Faolan?" Gwynneth asked gently.

"But what am I?"

"You are a wolf."

"A cursed wolf."

"Not cursed forever. You will prove yourself."

Faolan held up his splayed front paw. "This is why I am cursed."

"I know, your paw. I see it."

"No, you have not seen all of it. Take a closer look." Faolan flipped himself onto his back and showed the bottom of his paw, the pad with the spiral marking. He saw Gwynneth flinch, and flipped instantly back to his feet. *I am worse than* malcadh. *Much worse!*

But Gwynneth hopped closer to him and spread her immense wing over his head, patting him gently as she combed a burr from his ear with her beak. "You are a good wolf, Faolan. You are a good and honorable wolf. Both of your milk mothers would be proud of you."

He looked into the Masked Owl's dusky face. Her eyes were like gleaming blue-black river stones. They were darker than Thunderheart's, but he could see his reflection in them as he had once seen this face shining in Thunderheart's eyes. Faolan suddenly realized that this was his first conversation with any living creature since Thunderheart. It felt good. It felt comfortable. He sensed that he could say anything to this owl and that she would understand. The fire that had scared him at first now wrapped him in its warmth.

CHAPTER TWENTY-TWO

"You Must Go to the Wolves"

"MAY I STAY WITH YOU? I CAN hunt. I can get you big meat. Not just these little voles." Faolan nodded toward the bodies of the small rodents he saw stashed under a rock.

Gwynneth swiveled her head slowly, a wide arc that was almost a complete circle. But the meaning of the gesture was clear: *No!*

"What do I need with anything bigger than a vole? I am small compared to you. I can't get off the ground if I weigh myself down with too much food."

"But I want to stay."

"You belong with the wolves. You *are* a wolf."

"You don't want me." He stepped back.

"It's not a question of me wanting you or not." This was slightly untrue, but it was difficult to explain to a social animal like a wolf. Owls, especially Rogue smiths,

168

were known for their solitary ways. So she simply repeated, "You belong in a pack."

"On the fringes of a pack."

"Not always. No. You'll learn. You will gradually find a place in the pack and most likely will become a member of the Watch at the Ring of the Sacred Volcanoes."

"I know nothing about the ways of wolves and I am sick of this Sacred Volcano stuff," Faolan snarled.

"What do you mean sick of it? You don't know anything about it."

Faolan lowered his head and shifted his gaze. It was his turn to not be completely honest. He had not told Gwynneth about the Cave Before Time and now he was unsure if he ever would.

"If only Thunderheart were here."

"She's not. She's gone on." Gwynneth now flipped her head up so it was upside down and backward, and scanned the sky for the Great Bear constellation. It made Faolan dizzy just to see this extraordinary move.

"How do you do that?"

"Do what?"

"That thing with your head."

"We — owls, that is — have extra bones in our neck. It allows us to spin and twitch our heads every which way." Gwynneth began to demonstrate.

"Don't!" Faolan growled. "It's making me nauseous."

"Sorry! But as I was saying, Thunderheart is gone now. You can't recapture that time." Gwynneth spoke firmly, restoring her head to a fairly normal position with her eyes looking straight at Faolan.

Faolan huffed. Hadn't he done that in the cave? He had gone back to a time before time. He thought of those two owls separated by time: one plunging in what appeared to be a suicidal dive into the crater to retrieve the enigmatic ember; the other flying through a curtain of flames with the ember in its beak.

"But I can," Faolan said softly. *Can't I?* he thought.

"You must not think of time as a quantity, a period, a measure. Look at the sky," Gwynneth said. "The moon has now slipped away to another night, into another world. It was not the time it was here that you remember, Faolan, but rather the luminescence of the air, the blue shadows cast by the trees in its light. It was not the length of the time but the quality of the moon's light that you felt and remember." Gwynneth paused. "It is the value, the quality that lives on."

"But the moon will be back tomorrow and tomorrow and tomorrow and Thunderheart will not. It — it . . ." Faolan stuttered. "It's not fair."

Gwynneth puffed up to twice her size. She stepped so close to Faolan that her beak almost touched his nose. "You are too fine a wolf to think in such a small, selfish, stupid manner!" She lifted one wing and whacked him on the head. He sprang back. "Now you must go. Go to the wolves."

"I know nothing about them!"

"You know more than you think," Gwynneth said, her voice gentle again.

"Can I visit you?"

She sighed. "Not until you come back the gnaw wolf of a pack." The soft gray shadows before the dawn were thickening. "Now I must go to sleep. It's almost twixt time."

"Twixt time? What's that?"

Gwynneth yawned sleepily. "Twixt time is that minute between the last vanishing drop of the night and the first rosy drop of the dawn. We call it twixt time and if I don't get to sleep before that rosy drop, it's very hard for me."

"You sleep in the day?" Faolan was startled.

"Um-hm." Gwynneth nodded, her eyes half closed. "Such are the ways of owls."

Faolan sighed. The world seemed very complicated.

Owls slept during the day, bears through the winter. Would wolves have a new way of sleeping? What did he know about anything?

The fire was turning cold. The day growing lighter and emptier. Once more, Faolan felt a desperate desire to recapture time. Maybe Gwynneth was right. Time could not exactly be measured, not that warm time he had spent with her in a cocoon spun of firelight and star shine, of the crackles and hiss as the flames danced in their own hot wind.

He heaved himself up and, with the bone of Thunderheart in his jaws, he began to walk away. Never had he felt so lonely.

CHAPTER TWENTY-THREE

INSPIRATION

AFTER MANY HOURS OF SLEEP, Gwynneth felt the world growing darker. Tween time was approaching. The bright shadows that danced on the inside of her eyelids were beginning to turn a dusky violet. And although she still slept, something stirred in her, a gentle alert that the darkness all owls loved was approaching. Though her body remained motionless in the niche across from her forge, a part of her began to rise in a dream flight. Not a feather moved, and yet a whisper of wind lofted her toward that border between sleeping and waking. Then, precisely at the moment of true twilight when the sun dropped beneath the horizon, Gwynneth woke up. Her first thought was *Has he gone?*

She peered out from the stone niche and then stepped into the evening, spinning her head almost completely around. There was no sign of him. She felt a mixture of ease and sadness. She was relieved to be alone again, but she had to admit that she had found the young wolf's company a pleasure. The wolf was companionable and intriguing, and certainly the mark on the splayed paw was puzzling. The thought of it brought a little twitch to her gizzard.

Gwynneth reflected for several moments about the design on the paw and then with one talon tried to draw that design in the hard dirt near her forge. She wondered what the significance was of those spiraling lines. But even more unfathomable to Gwynneth was her shock upon seeing the spiral, like a bolt of lightning that seemed to flash through her gizzard. Why? What possible meaning could it have for her?

She poked at the fire a bit and then picked up the misshapen metal that she was trying to forge into a willow leaf. But those swirling lines filled her mind's eye and soon she realized that the elongated oval of the willow leaf was being stretched into another shape. She had not been aware that she had been slowly twirling the tongs as she held the piece in the fire to heat it. It had just seemed a comforting motion, almost hypnotic, as her mind had considered the pattern on Faolan's paw. The hunk of metal that had been roughly the shape of a leaf assumed a conical shape, and then, as the Rogue smith accelerated the twirling motion of the tongs, twists began to ripple from the point of the cone toward the base.

Quickly, Gwynneth drew the molten form out of the fire and began to tap the indentations between the rippling twists with her smallest hammer. She became more and more excited as she saw what was happening. It was as if she didn't even have to think, as if her talons had a direct connection to her gizzard. She worked ceaselessly, with a deeper concentration than she had ever experienced. Fluidly, she moved from one task to another as an extraordinary object began to emerge. She had to adjust the heat of the fire constantly by either blowing more air into it with bellows or damping it by shoveling dirt on top. After every few blows of the hammer, she plunged the object into a tub of water and then instantly back into the fire so that the metal would anneal properly. The rhythms of cooling and reheating for such a delicate object were complicated. If not done properly, the internal stresses of the metal would cause the object to break. But finally the piece was finished.

She held it up, still glowing cherry red — the only light in the foggy night aside from the forge fire. She blinked, looking at the spiraling coil as it cooled in the misty evening. It was a three-dimensional replica of the spinning lines on Faolan's footpad. "How did I do this?" she whispered in amazement. It was the most intricate piece she had ever made.

She churred softly to herself, for Gwynneth knew she would have never dared to attempt such a feat if she had known what she was doing, if she had planned it as she had planned the willow leaf. This was a hundred times more challenging than the leaf. *How in the name of Glaux did I do this?* she wondered. *And why?*

She now felt an urge to search for the wolf, to try to pick up his tracks. Not that she intended to meet up with him, but she was eager to see if he had heeded her advice and sought out the wolves of the Beyond.

The weather was coming in from the west. The stars and moon were obliterated behind woolly clouds and a thickening fog. Nights like these were often used by owls in covert tracking operations, as they could conceal themselves in the dense cloud cover and track by sound alone.

Masked Owls were members of the Barn Owl family, a species renowned for its auditory skills. A Barn Owl's ear slits were placed on either side of its head, one higher than the other. This uneven set of the ears helped the owls to capture sound better. But of additional value, the edges of the owls' facial disks had muscles that allowed them to expand their surfaces. This helped the owls scoop up any sounds and guide them to their ears.

It was not long before Gwynneth found the sound she had been searching for — the footfalls of Faolan. He had a distinctive rhythm because of the malformation of that forward paw. The spiral pattern in that paw wasn't engraved deeply enough to leave a print except perhaps in very fresh mud, but Gwynneth thought she could almost hear a sound print from the spiral.

She knew exactly where he was now. The wolf was clawing his way up the rocky scrabble of Bent Wing Ridge.

Good! she thought. *He's smack in the middle of the MacAngus territory.* She suspected he had been born into the MacDuncan clan. But it didn't matter. Angus MacAngus would see that he got back to the MacDuncans, if that was his clan.

But never a MacHeath, Glaux forbid he should be a MacHeath!

CHAPTER TWENTY-FOUR

THE RIDGE

THE OWLS CALLED THE RIDGE THE Bent Wing because the two parts of it joined at an odd angle to form an off-kilter wingspread. The wolves called the ridge Crooked Back and the highest part of it they called the Spine.

On the first morning after Faolan had left Gwynneth, he had picked up the wet odor of the caribou. And almost immediately he heard the wolves begin to howl. He listened carefully to what he guessed must be the *skreeleen*, the lead howler, announcing that meat was nearing. Gwynneth had told him about *skreeleens*. She explained how some *skreeleens* only howled about matters of prey and hunting, while others devoted their howling to relaying information about pack location back to the clan. Gwynneth had said that although she understood the wolves' howling generally, she never knew the precise meaning of the message.

But Faolan understood exactly what this *skreeleen* was communicating. It was the arrival of a large herd from the northwest. It was traveling at *tock-tock* pace. *Tock-tock* was a slow but steady speed in which the clicking of the caribous' tendons was still distinct, not a blur of sound as when the caribou ran very fast. It was the *tock-tock* speed that caribou used for long distances. Faolan could hear there were several new calves, a half dozen elderly caribou, at least three young bucks, and one young cow.

It was not long after the *skreeleen*'s message that the first of the caribou herd came into view. Faolan spotted four wolves loping almost lazily along the edges of the herd. He marveled that the herd had not panicked at the wolves' presence. Perhaps the wolves were feigning disinterest. Faolan was still high in the rimrock. He began to weave through the shadows as he monitored the wolves watching the caribou. He noticed the few subtle signals pass among these four wolves — a yelp, a flickering of ears, a head toss. Soon, two of the wolves peeled away from the herd. It wasn't long before they returned with the rest of the pack. The caribou immediately increased their speed. And then the scene became an exact replica of what Faolan had studied so closely on the rock walls in the Cave Before Time. Four females began pressing in on the herd, nipping at the flanks of the caribou on the outside edges.

Swiftly, the herd split. The female wolves in front of the formation of the pack began to bear down on two elderly bucks. Faolan watched it all. Eight females nipped at one buck's heels, trading off in alternate spurts of speed to conserve their own energy, yet keep the caribou pressed to the limits of his own endurance.

Faolan had brought down a caribou using his own ingenuity and what he had remembered from the cave paintings. But he had been alone. There was an incomparable beauty to what he saw now: the pack working together, smoothly, flawlessly. The splendor of it called to him. He did not know it, but the wolves had a word for what Faolan was seeing: *hwlyn*, spirit of the pack. Faolan craved that which he could not name.

Faolan watched the wolves for several days after that first morning. For the most part, he kept to the ridge, conducting his surveillance with extraordinary caution. He stayed downwind of the wolves.

The ridge ran for a great distance above a valley that

was a thoroughfare for many clans of wolves. It seemed to Faolan that normal territorial rules were not observed here. There were practically no scent markings, which must mean that it was open hunting to all clans.

He spotted something and crept down closer. It was the first time that he had seen a pack with what he thought might be a gnaw wolf.

He wanted to watch carefully and see exactly what this meant. Gwynneth had said a gnaw wolf's time in the pack was hard. The wolf had to prove itself.

The pack had brought down a moose just before he spotted them. Faolan watched closely as two members, a she-wolf and a male, approached the carcass slowly, almost reverently, and then sank to their knees and began to tear at the belly and the flanks, the tenderest parts of the animal. After they had eaten for a bit, the male raised his head and nodded toward four others of the pack who now walked toward the carcass. The gnaw wolf, a small yellowish wolf, hung behind. And not only did it stay back, one of the other wolves gave it a sharp head butt and a nip that sent the gnaw wolf yowling. The she-wolf who had eaten first raced over to the gnaw wolf, peeling back her lips in a ferocious low growl. The gnaw wolf flattened himself on the ground, rolling back his eyes until the whites shone like the gauzy shadows of two moons in the daylight. He yelped and whined pitifully.

The other wolves ate and ate. The gnaw wolf began to creep a bit closer, always slithering forward on his belly. If he got too close, a wolf broke away from its gorging and charged the gnaw wolf, snarling.

Will he ever get to eat? Faolan wondered. *How long must he wait?*

But while the wolves' treatment of the gnaw wolf was harsh, they did not seem vicious like the wolves of the Outermost. There seemed to be some greater purpose to their actions. But it was nonetheless mysterious. Finally, when the pack wolves had eaten their fill, a silent signal was given and the gnaw wolf approached. There was hardly a shred of meat left on the moose carcass. The she-wolf who had eaten first trotted up to where the gnaw wolf was trying to salvage a bloody tendril. She gave him a soft head butt and disgorged a pile of steaming moose flesh. The gnaw wolf groveled, mewled, and whined his gratitude. To Faolan, the groveling was the most revolting part of it all.

Not every pack had a gnaw wolf, which seemed fortunate to Faolan after witnessing the treatment of the small yellowish wolf. He saw similar scenes over the next few days. It was hard for him to reconcile or make sense of the gnaw wolves' treatment with what Gwynneth had told him of the exalted status they could attain when they became members of the Watch at the Ring of the Sacred Volcanoes. They seemed to be utterly despised by the others in the pack.

Faolan asked himself the same question over and over. *What kind of life am I going to? To be alone or be reviled, is there no other choice?* He did not want to be part of a pack if it was only to be the object of their cruelty. And yet he had seen something else when he had observed those wolves hunting. It was the matchless splendor of a pack working together, the inexpressible, amazing unity for which there was a single word, *hwlyn*, that Faolan had never heard but the meaning of which he sensed. It was the lure of that unnamable spirit of *hwlyn* that would finally draw Faolan down from the ridge. And yet something always stopped him just as he was about to bound down the steep slope of the ridge and reveal himself to a passing pack.

Faolan had ample opportunity to observe the different packs that composed the various clans. One pack seemed about the same as the other. He had no real preference, except he would prefer to avoid one clan. They seemed the closest to the wolves of the Outermost. The pack leaders of this clan did not confine their abuse to the gnaw wolves, but seemed to fight frequently among themselves. The MacHeaths were especially vicious toward the females, and he did not want to join them.

There was another clan that he noticed was mostly females, led by the only female chieftain he had observed so far. She was a tawny golden-colored wolf of some years. Her name was Namara, as he had learned through the howlings of the *skreeleens*.

The territory Faolan traversed was dominated by the MacAngus clan. It was the MacAngus clan who animated for Faolan the scenes he had observed in the paintings from the Cave Before Time. He had seen members of various MacAngus packs ever since he had arrived on the ridge and because of this he had stayed high near the rimrock that afforded a dense fringe of jagged shadows.

He had quickly learned how to thread his way through the shadows to conceal himself. It didn't take him long to learn what he thought of as the rhythm of shadows. It was in the mornings and the evenings that the shadows of the sun were the longest. This was convenient because it was midday when the wolves often rested.

In his time haunting the shadows, Faolan felt as if he were straddling two worlds with paws in each. In one world, he was on the edge of a beautiful dream, part of that painted pack on the cave walls, a fleet member of the flowing line of wolves. In the other world, the unpainted one he observed from the spine of the ridge, he was a young gnaw wolf waiting patiently at the far edge of the pack for his turn to eat. It seemed grossly unfair, for he had seen that little wolf run despite his twisted leg, seen it scurry around to block the caribou's way when it tried to head off in another direction. And yet he had to satisfy himself on mere scraps. But this was the way of the clans.

The season of autumn storms had arrived. On nights when the weather was most miserable he dared to go closer. There were torrential downpours, and when the sky was splintered with thunder and lightning, the wolves would gather in caves and a *skreeleen* would "read the sky fire."

One evening when thunderbolts fractured the sky, Faolan dared to come closer than he ever had before. The lightning *skreeleen* told a story of a chieftain from the time of the Long Cold who had grown old and toothless with age and lost his hearing, and whose eyesight had dimmed.

In the tradition of old wolves, he had gone out to a remote place to begin the steps of *cleave hwlyn*, the act of separating from his clan, his pack, and finally his own body. He had felt the marvelous sensation of slipping free from his pelt, becoming nothing more than a soft mist. He looked over his shoulder at his pelt glistening in the moonlight. His bones lay silent and cold, and he was bemused to realize how little they mattered to him. He sprang forward with the energy of a pup, leaping for the first rungs in the star ladder to the spirit trail leading to the Cave of Souls at the far point of the Great Wolf constellation.

He had made it halfway up the star ladder when the skies began to rumble. There was a sharp crack. A hot white line flared and the sky split in two. The star ladder shook and the old chieftain felt himself falling . . . falling . . . falling. He pawed the air with his claws, trying to cling to the star ladder. But the ladder had disappeared. There were no stars, only the storm-shattered blackness of the night branded with slivers of lightning. The sound was deafening and the world too bright. *How can this be?* thought the old chieftain. *I am deaf already and nearly blind!*

When the chieftain looked about, there was not a trace of his old pelt or his bones. He looked down. His paws were not misty, but planted firmly in the mud. He lifted one and stared in wonder at his paw print in the mud. *I am not old, but young. I am here on earth and not in the Cave of Souls. My time has not come.*

And then from the cave where the pack was hunkered down came a chorus of howls in response to the *skreeleen*.

"And that is why," the pack howled, "our chieftains wear pelts and necklaces of bones in honor of the great chieftain Fengo, who led us from the Long Cold. For that was the reason Fengo lived again."

Through the bolts of thunder
our history is read.
A threshold between two lands,
the living and the dead.
Forsake the starry ladder,
the cave of our souls,
Bring pelt and bone together.
The work is not yet done,
heed the call of Fengo
toward the setting sun.

The song of the wolves stirred something deep and mysterious within Faolan. He understood the words of the song, but there was something beyond the simple meaning that eluded him. When the song ended he had turned to leave. But the wind blew whisperings from the cave toward him. The pack sounded frightened. "Dangerous." "An enemy's coming." "Stranger. Beware."

What are they scared of? Faolan wondered. *They are a strong pack. Safe in the cave, heavy with fresh meat.* But he did not stay around to find out.

CHAPTER TWENTY-FIVE

MOON ROT
AND DOOM

THE RAINS HAD STOPPED FOR several hours when, after a long trek, Angus MacAngus, the clan chief of the MacAnguses, arrived at the cave where the pack of the western scree had spent the night of the storm. He had come in response to the *skreeleen's* howling. There were many interpretations that one could bring to the *ceilidh fyre*, or the sky dance of fire, as the wolves called lightning. It was disturbing that the *skreeleen* saw the story of the wolf who did not die, for it usually presaged misfortune.

The chieftain had not worn his ceremonial robes nor his necklace of bones. He did not want to make a fuss. It would alarm the pack unnecessarily if he had appeared in the elaborate garments usually worn in the *gadderheal*. They would think he found the situation so serious that they would all be summoned for a *gadder*. The *gadderheal* was the ceremonial cave of each clan where the gravest of matters were discussed.

The *skreeleen* came out to greet him. She was a handsome wolf, her silvery pelt glinting darker underneath. She lowered herself immediately to the ground, scraping her belly and grinding the side of her face into the dirt. Her ears were laid flat and her black lips drawn back in a classic gesture of total submission to her clan chief.

"No fire, Aislinn?"

"No, the dance did not cast a spark to the ground."

There were certain rules that governed conversation between the clan chieftain and the *skreeleen* who interpreted the *ceilidh fyre*. Although the chieftain was of higher rank than the *skreeleen*, he was not permitted to doubt her howled testimony. He was only allowed to ask for concrete signs or evidence that might support the grim possibility that the *ceilidh fyre* suggested. Even though the story of the wolf who fell from the star ladder was ultimately a heroic one, it involved much sadness and death. A fire ignited by a thunderbolt or even just a scorched rock would be considered most dire, a signal of an imminent calamity. The chieftain sniffed, trying to pick up any telltale scent of ash or fire. He widened his circle. The pack watched him carefully. A sudden shift in the wind brought with it a new scent. Angus MacAngus crinkled his brow and sniffed something.

"Any bears around here?" he asked.

"No, never," replied a high-ranking wolf. "They never come this far from the river."

"I don't understand. I smell bear, but wolf, too. No wolf from here, though."

"You smell two scents together?" asked the *skreeleen*.

"Yes, oddly mingled."

"As if they were traveling together? Walking side by side?"

Angus MacAngus stopped in his tracks and peered down at a strange paw print. His hackles rose stiffly, and he shoved his ears forward. So this was the misfortune foretold in the *ceilidh fyre*! The toe pads of the strange paw print were spread widely, splayed. It was the paw print of a wolf with the foaming-mouth disease. The sickness would end in death. But madness preceded the death and if the wolf encountered any other creature and bit it, that animal would go mad and die, too.

The bear scent made sense now. It was a grizzly sick with the disease, who had attacked and infected the wolf. Most likely the grizzly was dead by now, but the wolf prints were fresh. Something must be done.

Angus MacAngus turned and began to howl into the

summer morning, the shadow of the previous night's moon sailing overhead. Moon rot! An ill omen especially when coupled with the meaning of the *skreeleen*'s howling and the splayed paw print.

Angus knew he must alert the other clans of the danger. He must summon all the packs of the MacAngus clan and those of their neighbors, the MacDuncans, for a *gadderheal*. The word must be spread from the MacAnguses to the MacDuncans, from the MacNamaras to the MacDuffs and even to the loathsome MacHeaths. For this disease could spread faster than any howling. It might already be too late. The pack might be doomed. The clan might be doomed. Indeed, all the wolves of the Beyond could be annihilated.

And so the call went out, summoning the chieftains from the three nearest clans to a meeting in the MacAngus *gadderheal*. In the feeble trickle of moonlight, the chieftains made an eerie sight. Their own bodies seemed to have dissolved into wraithlike apparitions. Bedecked with headdresses and necklaces of gnawed bones, their shoulders were draped in cloaks from the pelts of animals, the ceremonial regalia required for meetings in the *gadderheal*.

A low ground fog obscured their legs so the wolf chieftains appeared to float across the landscape, their motion accompanied by the clinking of the gnawed bones.

Once inside the MacAngus *gadderheal* they paid obeisance to Angus MacAngus, lowering themselves until their bellies were flat against the ground. Although they were chieftains, tradition required that when called to the *gadderheal* of another chieftain, the visitor must acknowledge that clan's supremacy. Duncan MacDuncan, the eldest of the chieftains, began to lower himself painfully on arthritic legs.

"Enough, Duncan," Angus said softly. He then quickly turned to the others. "I have summoned you here because last night our *skreeleen* howled the *gwalyds* of the first Fengo."

Tension sizzled in the cave beneath the crackling of the flames in the fire pit.

Angus MacAngus huffed and continued, "And this morning I discovered a splayed paw print in the shadow of moon rot."

Loud gasps were followed by mutterings. "Terrible . . . terrible."

"It has been so long since the foaming-mouth disease came here."

"Not long enough," Duncan MacDuncan growled. "And we are far from any colliers or Rogue smiths," he added, staring into the fire pit. The wolves, unlike the owls of Ga'Hoole, had no skills with fire. The only fires they used were in their *gadderheals*. They bartered kill shares of meat for coals from Rogue smiths and colliers. There was, however, one other use for the coals in their pits, and that was to kill any animal afflicted with the foaming-mouth disease by driving it into the flames of a large fire trap. The first time they had used this strategy it had been easier to make the fire, for the diseased wolf had staggered into the region of the Sacred Volcanoes where hot coals and embers were plentiful. But now they were a vast distance from any such resource.

"There is always the Sark of the Slough," Duffin MacDuff said quietly.

A chill seemed to pass through the air at the mention of the strange wolf.

"A last resort," Drummond MacNab whispered.

"Is there any choice?" Angus McAngus asked.

"Falling star ladders, moon rot, doom, and the Sark of the Slough," MacDuncan muttered in his leathery voice. "I'd say not. No choice. No choice at all."

CHAPTER TWENTY-SIX

THE SARK OF
THE SLOUGH

THE WOLVES OF THE BEYOND, always concerned with order, believed that the system of rank and position that prevailed on earth corresponded to a superior one of the heavens. To disregard, upset, or affront this ranking could breed chaos in the world of wolves. There was a design to all set by Lupus, the heavenly spirit who glittered in the constellation of the Great Wolf. Lupus had set the design, and it must be followed.

The gnaw-bone necklaces that the wolf chieftains wore were not simply a symbol of their office, but a symbol of the Great Chain that linked the wolves to the heavens and reflected everything — soil, water, rock, air, and fire. The wolves divided living things into two classes: wolves and other animals. But within the classes there were other links in the chain extending down from Lupus.

This Great Chain was first described in the *gwalyds* of the early gnaw-bones, in descending order:

Lupus
Star wolves (the spirits of dead wolves who have
     traveled to the Cave of Souls)
Air
Ceilidh fyre (lightning)
Chieftains (clan leaders)
Lords (pack leaders)
Skreeleens
Byrrgis leaders
Captains
Lieutenants
Sublieutenants
Corporals
Packers
Gnaw wolves
Unranked Obeas
Owls
Other four-legged animals
Other birds, excepting owls
Plants
Earth Fire
Water

Rock

Soil

This order had been inscribed on gnaw-bones from time immemorial. It was, indeed, the first exercise that young gnaw wolves were put to after their return to a pack. They were required to spend endless hours on repeatedly gnawing the design of the Great Chain of the cosmic order that ruled the wolves of the Beyond. Wolves of the Outermost had flouted this order and had descended into chaos and discord. Even their howling reflected the dissonance of their lives.

But there was one creature who had not precisely flouted the order, yet dared to explore elements higher than she on the Great Chain. That wolf was the Sark of the Slough. She had become familiar with fire in a way that seemed to defy the order of things, and somehow neither commotion nor chaos had ensued. She was called a witch, or a Sark, for it was believed that she had special powers. She lived in a marshy region of the Beyond called the Slough. There, in a many-chambered cavern, she pursued experiments with what she called materials of the natural world.

That, in the eyes of the wolves of the Beyond, was the first insult. Fire was not of the natural world. It was from above and the only creatures who might consider it part of their world were owls, for they were also of air.

Of the wolves, only the Sark of the Slough had set herself to learn about fire. However, as soon as she had learned the rudiments of ember, coal, flame, and fire, she had kept herself apart from the owls. She was reclusive by nature. No one was sure where she had come from, nor did they know her clan ties.

There were, of course, rumors. Some said that she had been born so ugly, no wolf would mate with her. Considered barren, she might have been appointed Obea, but she had refused. It was then she had gone off to pursue her Sarkish practices and poke her snout into matters that were unnatural for a wolf. Others said that she had been born beautiful, so beautiful that her own mother, a she-wolf with Sarkish powers, had cast a spell upon her in a fit of jealousy that resulted in her hideous face.

Her face was not pretty, blighted by one eye that seemed to skitter a bit to the side. And her fur was wild, as if not just her hackles but her entire pelt was in a constant state of alarm. If one could look closely at her eyes — if indeed that one eye was not so skittish — one would see that her eyes were not the same color. One was the true green of the wolves of the Beyond, but the roving eye was amber colored, like the amber of an owl's eyes.

She was, in short, a freakish sort of creature. Of course, if she had had these defects at birth she would have been deemed a *malcadh* and been carried away by an Obea to be abandoned, and had she survived she would have become a gnaw wolf. But she was none of these and thus it was decided that she must be a Sark.

The Sark often muttered to herself as she pursued her experiments in her cave. She thought the other wolves' attitudes toward her a "grand silliness." There was nothing really witchy about her. She did not have powers. She had *ideas*.

She did not deal in evil charms. There was not an evil bone in her body, not an evil thought in her brain. In truth, she was a rather gentle wolf, and perhaps her greatest regret in life was not that she had never mated, but that she could not perform *lochinvyrr* as tidily as she might have liked because of her skittering eye. It was hard to look dying prey in the eye and acknowledge their lives as worthy when her eyeball was jumping about all over the place.

It would have been a shock to the other wolves that the Sark had any such emotions.

The wolves needed a Sark, because if there was one thing that fed the imagination of wolves as much as meat, it was the notion of strange, inexplicable powers. They weren't stupid, nor were they mean-spirited. But they were credulous, from the *skreeleens* with their half-baked star predictions to the chieftains with their elaborate rituals designed to rid the *gadderheals* of ill omens. The Sark did not know how she came by her decidedly practical and un-wolfish bent of mind.

She was contemplating all this as she tended one of the fires at the mouth of her cavern, preparing to mix henbane and mint to treat the scours that had afflicted a lone she-wolf. The wolf had been driven from her clan for giving birth to a *malcadh* just days before. She-wolves were frequently afflicted after losing their young.

This particular she-wolf had been cast out of the MacDuff clan. She was resting in one of the chambers deep in the cavern. The Sark often provided a halfway den for the grieving mothers. She hunted for them, gave them restorative tonics that she brewed up. The whole business that accompanied the birth of a *malcadh* was cruel, but one of the more practical customs of the clan wolves. It kept the clan healthy and maintained good bloodlines. It was usually possible for the cast-out parents to find new packs in other clans and new mates and produce healthy pups. This wolf would, too. The Sark would assure her of that in a few days, but it was too early now to broach the subject. The last thing this she-wolf wanted to hear about was a new pack, or a handsome recently widowed male wolf.

The Sark caught a whiff of something cutting through the aroma of the minted henbane, and stopped stirring. She walked outside the opening of the cavern to see the four chieftains approaching. "Oh, Great Glaux! What in the name of Lupus are the old codgers up to now?"

CHAPTER TWENTY-SEVEN

THE TRAIL OF THE SPLAYED PAW

"YOU SAY THE PRINT WAS TRULY distinct?"

"Indeed." The four chieftains nodded and replied in unison.

The Sark shook her head mournfully. She had no potions, medicines, or ointments for the foaming-mouth disease. The only way to stop it was to build a large fire and drive the foaming-mouth wolf into it. Of course she would help them.

She took her coal bucket, for which she had traded meat years before, and joined them. The Sark and the chieftains traveled together with some of their pack lords and officers, winding their way out of the Slough and onto the raised plains of the central plateau, where the chieftains had last seen the print of the splayed paw. They followed the track for the better part of the afternoon, but the Sark was growing uneasy. The print was not as clear as she would have thought, and most perplexing, it seemed that the wolf was favoring one paw, or at least that the other three left indistinct marks that could not be read as splayed. Was it that the sequence of footfalls was off? But she got no sense that the wolf was staggering.

It was slow going, as Duncan MacDuncan could not keep up on his arthritic legs. One corporal, a fast female, ran point. She was accompanied by two outflankers, also very fast females, who covered a wider swath on either side. There were back runners, too, both males, who looked for evidence that the foaming-mouth wolf was going back to cover its tracks. The Sark thought this was exceedingly stupid, as a wolf with foaming mouth became mad and would not have the sense to double back.

That was the other thing that disturbed the Sark. The foaming-mouth wolf's trail was straight, not erratic in a way that might suggest a crazed creature. But what disturbed the Sark the most was the splaying of that one paw. How could one paw be affected by the disease and not all four?

The outflankers had just returned with the news that the wolf had headed west toward the lagoons, shallow turquoise lakes rimed in salt.

"Good! Good!" exclaimed Angus MacAngus. "There is a defile near there that's perfect for building a fire trap. We'll send a team with you to help dig the trench." Angus MacAngus wheeled about and reared. "Laird, Mac, Brienne, you three head up the fuel collection." Then he turned to the other chieftains. "Will you honor us by appointing three mid-ranking in your clan to aid quartermaster Corporal Laird in fueling operations?"

Sark looked on, impressed by the crisp commands, the flawless organization. She had to credit them for their remarkable ability to marry the irrational messiness of their minds with the precision required of operational thinking. They were a wonder!

The Sark felt this might be the moment to introduce a reasonable question. She knew she would have to go through all the nonsense of those extravagant gestures of submission. What a pile of caribou poop!

But she folded her front knees under her chest and began lowering herself, peeling her lips back in a grimace of total humility. Sinking her head, grinding her jaw into the ground, and then twisting it so her good eye looked at the chieftain, she flashed it white in the final sign of humility. The skittering eye was hopeless at this sort of thing.

"Your question, Sark?"

"I would humbly beg to ask the outflankers for a description of the marks of the toe digs."

The chieftain nodded toward Finola. Cautiously, the wolf stepped forward. She was so frightened of the Sark that she trembled. "The toe digs were classic for a foaming-mouth creature. They dug deep into the ground, spaced perhaps twice or maybe even three times the normal width apart."

"All of the toe digs were as you describe?" the Sark asked. It was very hard to speak with half her face screwed into the ground, but the chieftain had not given her the sign to rise up as yet. He probably didn't want the outflanker to see her skittering eye. The poor thing was nervous enough as it was, and there was nothing like an amber-colored eye rolling about like some spoiled egg yolk to set a stomach churning.

"I am not sure what you mean by all the toes, uh . . . uh."

It was obvious that Finola was not certain how to address the Sark. The Sark held no rank. The Chieftain had called her Sark, but —

The Sark spared her the pain of this decision by asking another question. "I mean were the toe digs all from one paw? More precisely, we know that this wolf is on an easterly course. Which would mean that the splayed toe digs would flare south or north. Did you notice them all flaring in one direction?"

There was a long pause before Finola answered. "Well, now that I think about it, yes, the most distinct marks seemed to flare slightly to the south."

"None to the north?"

"Uh . . . uh . . . I'm . . ." she stammered. Finally, she said, "I cannot really say those marks were less distinct, but very possibly."

"Might this suggest that we are dealing with . . . well, not a clear-cut situation if only one paw seems to bear the symptoms of the foaming-mouth disease?"

"One paw, two, three, or four!" Duffin MacDuff stepped forward. "What does it matter? This disease means doom."

"Yes! Absolutely!" There was a chorus of huzzahs, cries of approval, and paw-pounding to signal the wolves' agreement with Duffin MacDuff.

The Sark sensed it was a lost cause, but she felt compelled to give reason one more try. "The evidence does not suggest that. I ask you to reconsider —"

Duffin MacDuff snarled and cut her off immediately.

"There shall be no more argument. We must proceed to build the fire trap immediately! The coals are still hot?" Angus McAngus asked.

"Yes, sir," the Sark answered grimly, peering down at the bucket which glowed orange-red with the hot embers.

"Then rise up and go to the salt lagoon defile."

CHAPTER TWENTY-EIGHT

JUMP FOR THE SUN

FAOLAN TROTTED UP A GENTLE incline to a promontory from which he could see two sparkling lakes. They twinkled like twin gemstones in the clear air. The sun, as luminous as the amber eye of an owl, was making its stately descent. Faolan was watching this spectacle when he had the sudden sensation that there was something on his trail. Oddly enough, the feeling was not unfamiliar. He realized that this sense of being followed had been with him for some time, perhaps since the sun had first risen.

He made for the lakes, but the sensation stayed with him.

Who could be tracking me? He crouched down to press his ear to the ground. The sound cut through him like fangs. This was not just a predator, nor was it a single animal. This was the sound of wolves, and not just a pack, but several packs. He closed his eyes, not able to quite believe what he was hearing. The painted image from the Cave Before Time flashed in his mind. Those *byrrgises* that he had seen and longed to travel with — *that will never be!*

The words dropped into his mind like pebbles in still water, the ripples radiating with the terrible truth. *I am the prey!* This was the sound of a *byrrgis*, and they were on his trail.

The sound was drawing closer. There was no time for anger, no time for regret. He had to use all his wits and all his muscle. Could he confuse wolves? Could he leave a false track somehow? But where? The landscape was barren. Could he circle back, loop around? Desperately he looked about and then he caught a glimpse of them just breaking over the bluffs behind him.

One wolf against a byrrgis! *I'm doomed!* He could hear their pace. It was not press paw yet. They did not go full out until they were close, to conserve their energy.

A frantic thought flashed into Faolan's mind. His chest was broader than many of the wolves he'd seen, not just the yearlings but the full-grown wolves, too. Thunderheart had made him jump and walk on two legs, and pressed him to eat the richest meat. Now he could take bigger, deeper breaths to propel himself forward. That would be his strategy. *Let them catch up to me on the flats, and I'll fool them into thinking they almost have me and then press paw on the hills.* There were several hills ahead; there was a slim chance he could out-run them.

But as he leaped forward, grief coursed through him. He could not believe that the wolves of the Beyond were trying to kill him. Gwynneth had been wrong. He cut off the thought and slowed. He could hear their panting now, and four long shadows stretched on either side of him. They were catching up. Just ahead was the first bluff. Faolan sprang forward as he reached the beginning of the incline and began to streak toward the crest. The sound of their footfalls receded. The shadows of the outflankers that had been closing in vanished. He knew there was another long flat stretch ahead where they would catch up again. Could he wear them out? How long could he spin out this game with them?

Faolan reached the flats all too soon. The wolves closed in on him again, steering him toward something brighter than the sun. Too late Faolan saw it, a wall of fire in the gap between the two lakes. It was a defile. They were hunting him as he and Thunderheart had hunted the caribou.

There was no sound except for the wolves breathing. He was being driven into a wall of fire. He could feel its heat reaching for him. An immense heat. He could hear it now. Crackling. Spitting. The fiery tongues licking the air, gulping, raging. Closer and closer he was driven. *I have no choice but to die.*

The words streaking through his mind angered him profoundly. The fire was upon him. The sun reeled in the sky as the word *NO!* exploded in his brain. He opened his jaws and his chest expanded with air, as if he were swallowing the sky. *I have jumped for a tree, jumped for a raven, jumped for a cougar. I shall jump for the sun!*

Overhead, the dark shape of an owl's wings cut the blueness of the sky. Gwynneth soared in growing alarm on the warm updrafts of the fire as she began to understand what was happening beneath her. She had seen the smoke from a distance and come to explore, for fire was an unusual occurrence in the region of the salt lagoons. She now hung on the warm ledge of air in horrified dismay. *It's Faolan, Great Glaux, it's Faolan! They think he has the foaming —*

She never finished the thought, plunging in what the

owls called a kill-spiral toward the wolves, screeching, "Stop! Stop!" But her cries were swallowed by the roar of the fire. And then her wings seemed to seize up, freeze. The wolves jolted to a stop as a silver streak arced over the wall of fire, clearing the highest flames.

"Yeep" was the name of the condition that had afflicted Gwynneth when her wings locked. Luckily, she recovered her wits before smacking into the ground. By the time she had regained her flight instincts, the wolves had begun to howl.

"Idiots! Absolutely idiots!" the Sark of the Slough fumed at the chieftains, who stood with their jaws gaping. The sight that they had just witnessed was one of terrifying beauty and grace. Had the wolf sprouted wings? How had he soared so high? It was easier to believe that he might have been scorched by the sun.

"Go ahead and howl, the lot of you! He no more has the foaming mouth than any of you! There was enough evidence. One paw splayed! Not two, not three. Not four, not . . . not eighteen!" the Sark roared in a thunderous baying.

Duncan MacDuncan limped forward.

"Bow down, bow down," a captain from the MacDuncan clan growled at the Sark. "Show your respect."

"No, no need! No one should perform the submission rituals," the old chieftain said wearily. "It is my fault. I'm too old to be chieftain."

"Oh, no. No," several wolves protested.

"Yes!" MacDuncan growled. "When your memory shreds and you forget that a year ago a *malcadh* was born with one splayed paw." A silence fell upon the wolves. MacDuncan looked about and nodded at a gnaw wolf, a yearling missing its tail and with a crooked hip.

"You have brought your bone?" Duncan MacDuncan asked.

"Of course, honorable chief." The young wolf named Heep sank to his knees and was grinding his face into the dirt.

"Rise up," Duncan MacDuncan snapped. "Stop venerating and start carving." He turned to the others and began to speak in a tremulous voice. "Let it be recorded on the gnaw-bone that in the moon of the frost blossoms, when the river ice still locked the water, a pup was born with one splayed paw to Morag and her mate, Kinnaird. The pup was taken by the late Obea, Shibaan,

213

to be abandoned. This pup did not die. This pup survived and has now earned its place as a gnaw wolf in the MacDuncan clan."

The gnaw wolf Heep slid his eyes around nervously as if looking for something and then returned to the bone. Duncan MacDuncan then turned to the Sark. "Where is that wolf now?"

"He's on the other side of the trap fire with Gwynneth," the Sark replied.

"Gwynneth, the Rogue smith?"

The Sark nodded.

"He survived the fire?" the chieftain asked.

"He did more than survive," the Sark answered acidly. "He jumped the wall of fire! You all saw him!" She tried to speak evenly, but she was seething with anger.

"He challenged the order," a wolf from the MacDuff clan whispered.

Heep looked up again, a glint now in his eyes. Into the bone he began to chisel with his teeth a design depicting the Great Chain. Cleverly, he placed the chain over a large crack in the bone, making it appear broken.

"Can you fetch him and bring him forth?" MacDuncan asked.

The Sark nodded. She soon came back with Faolan. He looked fresher than the outflankers who had chased him so hard. Standing bright and silver, a soft breeze stirred his pelt so that he appeared almost to shimmer. He sensed the wariness of the nearby wolves as he advanced. He kept his eyes forward, focused on the horizon and refused to even glance at the gathering of chieftains to whom he was being led.

Duncan MacDuncan stepped forward. The air began to buzz when the wolf with the splayed paw did not begin to lower himself to the ground, but Duncan MacDuncan took no offense. "Heep, come forward and read what you have recorded thus far in the gnaw-bone."

Heep quickly trotted up with the bone in his mouth, dropped it, and began an elaborate sequence of movements and postures that soon had maneuvered him into a state of flatness as if a boulder had crushed him.

"Honorable chieftain, highest lord of the MacDuncan clan, I offer what I have carved in respect and profound humiliation."

"Sycophants, the lot of them," the Sark whispered to Gwynneth.

"Just get on with it!" Duncan MacDuncan boomed.

So Heep began to read. He did not read the last symbols he had started to carve regarding the Great Chain. He had a feeling that this might not please Duncan MacDuncan.

"Bring the bone you just gnawed, Heep, and show this wolf your work."

"It is not quite finished, sir."

"No matter. I just want for this wolf to see examples of gnawing, for this will be his task."

Faolan walked somewhat stiff legged, his lip nearly cleared his teeth — a silent snarl threatening to break out. He was trying to sort out in his mind what exactly was happening. These were the wolves that had wanted to kill him and now they were staring at him with an odd mixture of wariness and deference. He wasn't sure what was expected of him. Gwynneth had briefly explained to him about the mistake. That they thought he had been afflicted with the foaming-mouth disease. But no one was saying they were sorry. There were no apologies being offered. Heep dropped the bone between Faolan and the chieftain.

Faolan looked at the bone carefully. He was not impressed. The lines were clumsy, the narration disorganized. There was one part that was not finished. Faolan had never even lived within a clan and yet the bones he had gnawed were much finer. He thought of the paw bone of Thunderheart on which he had gnawed their story, the story of that glorious summer, fall, and the winter den. He had buried that bone on the other side of the slope he had climbed to see the salt lagoons and had not had time to go back for it. But better that it was buried in a secret place. Better that this young gnaw wolf called Heep never see it.

He was suspicious. Suspicious of all these wolves. But something within him bade him to keep his thoughts to himself.

The chieftain turned to Faolan. "It takes a long time, a very long time to become a fine gnawer. Gnawing is an art. You now qualify to become gnaw wolf, and if you gnaw well, you may go on to join the Watch at the Ring of the Sacred Volcanoes. You will become a member of the clan of the MacDuncans. We shall soon decide which pack you may join, and name you."

The loneliness that had walked beside him for so long began not to recede, but to contract, to migrate from his side to that hollow within him where it had begun. Now, although he was surrounded by his own kind, he felt more estranged than ever, gaunt with his own loneliness.

So, Faolan thought, *I am to join a pack.* And a pack was part of a clan. *I am to become a wolf of the Beyond.* He looked now at these wolves, the chieftains, the outflankers, and the others who had comprised the *byrrgis* that had nearly killed him. Was there any wolf that looked remotely like him, one who could have been his mother or father, a sister, a brother? According to Gwynneth his own parents would have had to find new packs that were quite distant from their old one. But they would never have gone to the Outermost. As wary as Faolan now was, he knew that these wolves were decent creatures. They were not outclanners.

"You will join?" It was a question, not a command, that Duncan MacDuncan asked.

Faolan nodded.

"Do you understand?"

Faolan nodded again.

"Do you have any questions?"

Faolan hesitated. "Not a question, sir, but . . ."

"But what? A comment, perhaps?"

"Yes, a comment," Faolan said.

Again, there was a surge of whispers. "How dare he?" "A gnaw wolf doesn't have comments!" "He'll learn!"

"Go on," Duncan MacDuncan said softly.

"Sir, let the gnaw-bone show that I have a name."

"A name?" Duncan MacDuncan blinked. "How did you happen to come by a name?"

The question almost confused Faolan. His name wasn't an accident. Thunderheart had chosen it for him.

"I was named by my milk mother, the grizzly bear Thunderheart."

"Your milk mother was a *bear?*" MacDuncan staggered slightly.

"Yes. My name is Faolan. That is the name my milk mother, the grizzly bear Thunderheart, gave me." He turned his eyes toward the gnaw wolf Heep, then swept the assembled wolves in the green light of his gaze. "Call me Faolan."

The Outermost

Cougar
Tree

Cave
Before
Time

BEYOND
THE
BEYOND

MacI
Ter

Frost Forest

Winter den
of Thunderheart
and Faolan

Summer de
of Thunderh
and Faola

Salt Lakes

N

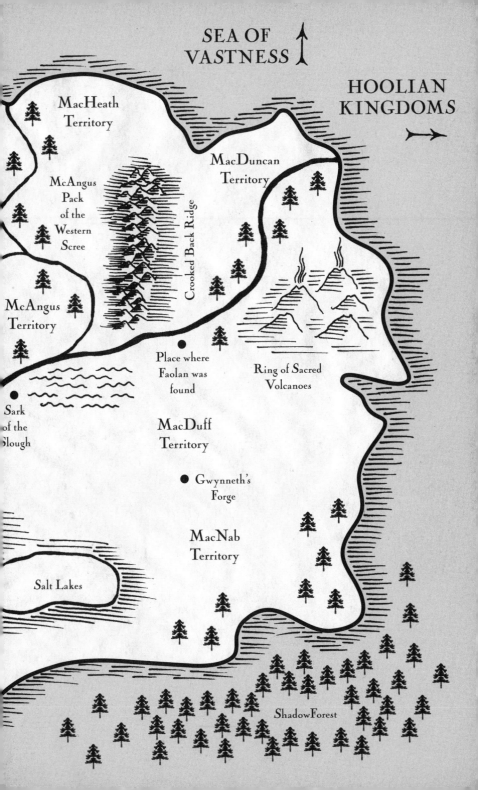

SEA OF
VASTNESS

HOOLIAN
KINGDOMS

MacHeath
Territory

McAngus
Pack
of the
Western
Scree

MacDuncan
Territory

Crooked Back Ridge

McAngus
Territory

Sark
of the
Slough

Place where
Faolan was
found

Ring of Sacred
Volcanoes

MacDuff
Territory

Gwynneth's
Forge

MacNab
Territory

Salt Lakes

Shadow Forest

This book was designed by Lillie Mear.

The text was set in 12.5 point Goudy Old Style.

The production was supervised by Joy Simpkins.

The book was printed and bound at

R. R. Donnelley in Crawfordsville, Indiana,

in the United States of America.

Manufacturing was supervised by Jess White.